Hello, Mr Magpie

Of course, every girl knows the only thing to do in a crisis is have your hair cut. My hair seems to be getting shorter and shorter and I'm in danger of being mistaken for a diesel dyke – so I'm overcompensating by wearing floaty, flowery dresses and very red lipstick.

I'd completely forgotten that I'm a sometime actress and when my agent rings (I'd completely forgotten I had one) to tell me she is finally retiring and she's sorry but she can't make alternative arrangements for me, i.e. from now on I will not only be jobless and agentless but completely prospectless too, I enter a depression blacker than the latest black top bought in the Joseph sale made from fabric apparently immune to bleach and therefore supposed to stay black forever.

Penny Faith was born in London in 1958 and despite changing her address a dozen or so times, has never lived too far from Hampstead Heath. She currently lives in East Finchley (a five minute drive from Kenwood) with her daughter Dodo, and her dog, Dusty.

Hello, Mr Magpie

Being the history of Ms Hattie Gordon
including her own thoughts and impressions

A novel
by
Penny Faith

FLAME
Hodder & Stoughton

Copyright © 1999 by Penny Faith

The right of Penny Faith to be identified as the Author of
the Work has been asserted by her in accordance with the
Copyright, Designs and Patents Act 1988.

First published in Great Britain in 1999
by Hodder and Stoughton
First published in paperback in 1999
by Hodder and Stoughton
A division of Hodder Headline

A Flame Paperback

10 9 8 7 6 5 4 3 2 1

A CIP catalogue record for this title is available
from the British Library

ISBN 0340 72841 8

Printed and bound in Great Britain by
Caledonian International Book Manufacturing Ltd.

Hodder and Stoughton
A division of Hodder Headline PLC
338 Euston Road
London NW1 3BH

Acknowledgements

This novel was public property from almost the very first words, so there are copious amounts of people whom I need to thank for their time taken either reading it or listening to me read it aloud, for their constructive criticism, but mostly for their belief that I had written something that had its place as a pebble on the mountain of published fiction. Special thanks for making it happen to Patrick Walsh, heaven must be missing an agent, and Carolyn Mays for making it all so simple.

So, with thanks to Sue Gee, the most positive and caring of tutors, for getting me started and all concerned with the BA in Writing and Publishing at Middlesex University; to the very wonderful friends I have made through The Splinter Group; Keith Charters for the relentless PMA, (I did do it), Ivy Ngeow (remember

the name), Clair Whiteman (you can read it now), Jane
Hoodless (you bully you) for being a lesson to us all,
Terri Paddock (looking forward to yours) and Chrissie
Underdown (hi Sonny) for being so generous with their
contacts, and our newer members Katy Massey who is
such a good listener and Hamish MacFarlane who is
such a good writer.

Then there's those who just seemed to know, Lucy
Aston, Tracey Fogg, Jo Marks and those who've thrilled
to the success, Glen Marks, Sara and Paul Robinson,
Alex and Philip Goodhand-Tait, Michael Vivian and Lee
Beaumont.

A huge thank you for the incredible support and
encouragement I have received from Archie Markham,
John Turner and Jane Rogers, the MA tutors at Sheffield
Hallam University, who more than anyone else have
helped me believe I am a writer, and all my fellow MA
students, too numerous to name who I understand are
mostly 90% pleased for me!

And finally a special BIG thank you to Dodo who's put
up with a mother who has been sometimes distracted
enough to send her to school without her swimming
things.

Permissions

❈

101 Dalmations by Dodie Smith is reprinted by permission of Egmont Children's Books Ltd

Extracts from 'The Movie Quote Book' reproduced by permission of the publishers, Omnibus Press

Extract from 'The Collected Plays of Noel Coward' reprinted by permission of the publishers, Methuen

Missis shook her head.
'It's hopeless,' she thought.
'How can I depend on
something that depends?'

Dodie Smith
101 Dalmations

Prologue

∞

'Hello, Mr Magpie, hello Mr Magpie, hello Mr Magpie.'

'Where?'

'Just flew up into that tree.'

'Damn. Missed it.'

'It doesn't matter.'

'What doesn't matter?'

'If you don't see it, you don't need to say anything.'

'Oh. There it is again.'

I watch the magpie swoop down from the low branches and make a perfect landing on the grass 50 yards away from our picnic. I am about to start my chant when a second magpie joins him.

'Phew!' I say.

Franny starts to laugh, 'I can't believe you sometimes.'

'Simon and I take our magpies very seriously. We always have done, haven't we Simon?'

Simon removes his lips from Kate's ear and mumbles a reply.

The birds fly away.

Seconds later one of them is back.

'10, 9, 8, 7, 6, 5, 4, 3, 2, 1,' says Grace, jumping up and spinning around.

Toby spits three times, 'Just to make sure.'

'This is ridiculous,' says Franny.

'But it's bad luck to see one on its own,' I tell her. 'You have to say something to counter it.' But before I can, it is gone again.

'Oh, for God's sake you lot. I mean, what's the worst that could happen?'

This is a fair question on a day when everything seems so perfect. From my position lying on the ground on my stomach leaning up on my elbows, occasionally raising a leg then dropping it, I look from one to the other and back again. These can be the best of times – all of us together. I watch the patterns of sunlight dance over the ground as a cooling, calming late summer breeze flows through leaves which will never be greener, never be lovelier.

'Not getting the part,' says Toby in response to Franny's question. He readjusts the headphones on his Walkman and continues practising his harmonies.

'Spurs winning—' says Adam. We await the end of the sentence. '—anything.'

'Yeah?' says Grace, her angry black eyes darting around at us. 'What about being cold, hungry, sick?'

'The worst that could ever happen,' says Simon, 'is that things change.'

'But all things inevitably turn into their opposites,' says Kate sleepily. 'It's a law of Physics.'

Day to night, hot to cold, Life to Death.

Love to indifference, laughter to tears, trust to betrayal.

I look over at Adam, his eyes closed and his head gently swaying as chemically induced thoughts slowly rot his brain.

'Or,' I say, 'that they never change.'

Black, white, blue crosses my eye line.

'OK. New rule. From now on every time we see a magpie on its own we count to three. If by then another one has failed to appear, then we can say it.'

I watch the lone magpie glide around looking for its partner.

'1, 2, 3. Right. Hello, Mr Magpie. How's your lovely wife?'

Chapter One

In which our heroine comes face to face with a rat, experiences her first kiss, tells a filthy joke and gets the once-over from her future mother-in-law

It's time to empty the bowl that has been sitting by the sink collecting tea bags, potato peelings and apple cores, in my one concession to organic gardening.

On the way to the compost heap I stop to admire my favourite sight in the garden – drops of water settled in the centre of lupin leaves, perfectly still, clear and round like some special kind of magic contact lens that you know won't fall out at an inappropriate moment. Lucky lupins.

At the pile of rotting waste I do a double-take. Did I or did I not see a long, thin, slimy thing bearing an uncanny resemblance to a rat's tail, slithering under last week's dead flowers? The rat's tail is remarkably smooth and shiny and totally unlike the simile that Mother called upon so frequently to describe my unbrushed hair.

I pick up the bamboo stick waiting to provide support for the climber *(Cobaea scandens)* propagating in a pot on the kitchen windowsill, and tentatively poke around in the compost heap. I am standing well clear, plus the length of the stick, so when the unsightly rodent's face appears baring a grin that would put Tom Cruise to shame, I have a good head start and sprint into the kitchen, close the door quickly and lean against it.

I hope to God the rat does not suddenly appear at the window, like Patrick Bergin in *Sleeping With the Enemy*.

I put the kettle on to make a cup of calming tea and pick up a copy of *Time Out*.

The magazine completely infuriates me. I have no idea why I continue to buy it. Its only use is for telephone numbers of cinemas to find out the showing times of films and any number of publications could offer me that. But I still continue to buy *Time Out*. It reminds me of my marriage to Adam, except by the end I could not think of a single reason still to be in it or a single use for my husband – certainly nothing as vital as a cinema's telephone number.

The phone rings. I go into the living room to answer it. It is Kate; still no sign of the imminent birth.

I return to the kitchen to resume my co-dependent relationship with the listing magazine, but cannot find it anywhere. I turn over piles of last Sunday's papers, two weeks' worth of undealt with mail and the pile of newly acquired paperbacks (bought at a discount – one of the few advantages of my part-time job at the book shop) but cannot find *Time Out* anywhere.

Perhaps the rat has stolen it.

1990
The 'what-are-we-going-to-eat?' game

It's like this most weekends.

'What are we going to eat?' asks Grace.

'I could go to Ridley Road,' says Adam.

'We had that last Sunday,' I say. 'There's still chopped liver in the fridge.'

'No, I don't fancy that,' says Toby.

'What do you fancy?' I ask him.

'I don't know,' he replies. 'But not that.'

'When's Jan coming?' I ask.

'Anytime,' says Grace.

'Maybe we should wait for her.'

'I think I'd like a kebab,' says Kate.

'Anyone want a cup of tea?' asks Adam.

'Yes, I could go for a kebab,' I say.

'Yeuch,' says Grace. 'No thanks.'

'What do you mean "yeuch"?' Kate asks her.

'I mean I don't want one.'

'Well, that doesn't make them "yeuch" just because you don't want one. What about a pizza?'

'I hate pizzas,' says Toby.

'Since when?' I ask.

'Another beer anyone?' asks Adam.

'You don't hate pizzas,' I tell Toby.

'It depends where they come from,' he says.

'We only order nice pizzas in this house,' I say.

'I just don't feel like one,' says Toby.

'What do you feel like?' asks Kate.

'I don't know,' says Toby.

'Another line anyone?' asks Adam.

1974
Wasn't my fourteenth birthday party the one with the dead cat?

Adam Levy and I are standing behind the tulip tree. It is very wide and very tall and very rare. There are only half a dozen or so tulip trees in the whole country, and one of them is in our garden. I am leaning against the trunk and Adam is hovering in front of me.

He takes my hands then drops them, deciding instead to put his hands on my shoulders. Having done that, he can now pull me towards him. As he does so he closes his eyes. I don't. I want to watch. I watch his face looming nearer and nearer, his lips part slightly, then suddenly I can see no more because his face is right on top of mine. His lips touch my lips and move slowly around

4

them, then he applies slight pressure and they stop moving. The pressure increases.

I wonder what on earth he thinks he is doing.

His arms have moved to encircle my neck. My arms hang limply by my sides.

He decreases the pressure on my lips and starts to move around them again. Then he pulls away and leaves a single kiss on my now-experienced mouth.

He smiles and winks one wild green eye.

The moment is broken by a loud scream and half a dozen other fourteen-year-olds come running into view.

Adam moves away from me abruptly.

'What's going on?' I ask.

'Oh, Hattie, it's disgusting,' says Margie.

'What is?'

'That horrible dog of yours,' she replies.

'What?'

'Look,' she says.

I come out from behind the tree. There, in the middle of the lawn, are the decaying, mud-covered remains of a once-black cat. Dexter, earth all over his nose, is standing over it proudly wagging his tail. I go over to him.

'Dexter,' I say reproachfully, 'did you bring me a birthday present?'

1971
The first time I met Margie the Minx

As we come out of the headmaster's office I notice her sitting there, trying not to look like I felt twenty minutes or so ago. Our parents smile at each other. We do not. I am uncomfortable in school regulation grey pleated skirt, white blouse, navy jumper and navy blazer. She is more relaxed in her own clothes – white wet-look miniskirt, matching boots, tight black ribbed polo neck.

I can feel Mother's crossness even before she speaks.

'Why did you tell him you were reading a comic book?' she asks. She cannot contain herself to wait until we are alone.

'Because it is. It's a funny book. So it's comic. You know a comic book.'

'But now he thinks you read comics.'

Mother is in despair. You see, if the headmaster does not discover that I am very probably one of the few eleven-year-olds he has ever met who has read the whole of Jane Austen, he may not offer me a place in his school. Besides, had she forgotten the regular arrival of Bunty along with Wednesday's Daily Mail?

'I don't know why you're reading that book anyway,' she adds, just to try and make me feel even smaller.

I attempt a distorted smile at my peer, but she does not respond. Taking in her parents, her father looking like Tony Curtis, her mother like Lana Turner, I can't imagine her suffering similar torments.

The headmaster appears silently, as headmasters do, from his office. He seems surprised to still see us there.

'Margaret Rowan?' He addresses the pretty blond girl. She stands up, acting coyly, her clear blue saucer eyes peering up through long lashes.

'Everyone calls me Margie,' she says with frightening confidence.

'All right then, Margie. Please come in,' he says, holding the door open for her and her parents to pass through.

Before she disappears she turns to look at me with a challenging glare, but before I can decipher its meaning Dad says, far too loudly, 'They're going to have trouble with that one.'

1972
I can't believe she said that

Margie is coming to my house for tea. She has made sure she is seated next to Simon in the back of the car.

Mother keeps glancing into her rear-view mirror to check on Margie's activities. Fortunately my brother is immune to Margie.

We are forced to stop to allow a coach to unload its cargo of boys back from the playing fields, into a nearby school.

My mother groans with frustration. Margie squeals with delight.

'Ooh, look at all those lovely boys,' she says.

'Hattie doesn't think so,' snaps my mother.

Simon and I look at each other. I shrug my shoulders as if to say, 'I have no idea why she said that.'

Anyway, she's wrong.

'What's the filthiest joke you know?'

'What?'

Luke takes his right arm from the back of my neck, turns on his side towards me, leans up on his elbow, then runs his left hand down from my lips to my navel, finally letting it rest on my stomach.

'What's the filthiest joke you know?'

'I don't know,' I say.

'Go on, I want to know.'

How is it you can share your body with someone you hardly know, yet get embarrassed about telling a dirty joke?

'OK. Um. Little Red Riding Hood is going to visit her grandmother who lives at the other side of the forest—'

'I know where Red Riding Hood's grandmother lives,' interrupts Luke.

I look at him.

'Only teasing,' he says, giving my stomach a light pinch. 'Go on.'

'When suddenly this wolf jumps out from behind a tree. "Where are you going, little girl?" asks the wolf—'

'Maybe you should do a wolf voice there.'

'What? Oh, professional advice. Right.' I deepen my voice, '"Where are you going, little girl?" "I'm going to visit my grandmother who lives at the other side of the forest."' I put on a high-pitched little girl's voice.

Luke laughs. 'That's good,' he says.

'"Oh no you're not," says the wolf,' I continue, '"because I'm going to gobble you up." "Gobble, gobble, gobble," says Little Red Riding Hood. "Is that all you do? Don't you ever fuck?"'

'I'm shocked.'

'No you're not.'

'Oh, yes I am.'

'You asked for a dirty joke.'

'What I'm shocked about is that you think that's dirty. Now if you want to hear a really filthy joke—'

There's no point in getting all dressed up for this one. They're looking for a young mother. They don't want to see you top to toe in Armani; Marks & Spencer is the look they're going for. But I want to be a bit smart, so I wear my black Jigsaw lycra-mix trousers, black loafers, brown body and black M & S blazer. I love putting brown and black together, strictly against the advice of the fashion magazines.

I see a few familiar faces. We all look pretty much the same. I don't know how they choose between us. It's always the same people at the castings and it's always the same people in the ads.

'Hattie Gordon?'

It's my turn. I enter the office. Three people sit behind a desk. A camera dominates the centre of the room. I am asked to sit on a chair in front of it.

None of them directly address me except to ask me to turn my left then right profile. They discuss my CV between them, but not with me. I know I won't get this one so I just want this ordeal to be over as quickly as possible. I try to relax and smile and look as happy as a young mum would serving fish-shaped breaded fish to her ravenous just-returned-from-a-hard-day-at-school child.

At last I am freed.

Later my agent rings me.

They want to see me again.

Sadie is giving me the 'isn't-it-time-you-did-something-with-your-life?' speech. Apart from the discomfort of confrontation, I am puzzled as to what authority she has to do this. So I ask her.

'What gives you the right to talk to me like this?'

'We're concerned.' She's dangerously close to treating me like one of her charity cases.

'Oh, it's "we" is it? And where is "we"?' I act searching around the room. 'This isn't coming from Simon. Simon would never speak to me like this. It's you who can't accept me, not him.'

'Simon is concerned.'

'About what exactly?'

'We just want you to be happy again. You used to be so happy.'

Boy, has she got a nerve.

'I'd sure hate to have your nerve in a tooth,' I say.

Sadie glares at me.

'You always do that. Both of you.'

'What?'

'You know, resort to lines from movies. Trivialise. Turn everything into a joke.'

There is real disdain in her look. But then she relaxes.

'Look, Hattie,' she starts again.

I can't bear that tone.

'It's all right for you,' I begin, but Sadie isn't buying that one.

'What? What is all right for me? Just because I haven't got a failed marriage and a failed career, that doesn't mean I haven't got any problems.'

I can't believe she said that.

'It must be really tough being married to my brother. I mean, he's generous, supportive, loyal, but . . . he quotes movies at you.'

Sadie collapses back on her sofa.

'I tried, I really tried,' she says.

'I don't know why you bothered,' I say. 'Actually, I'm fine. And I don't need to prove it to you.'

Sadie sits up wearily.

'I've got to pick up the kids. You coming?'

'I think I'll go home,' I say. 'Give them a kiss from me.'

'Sure,' she says.

I arrive at the Bookshop ten minutes early. George looks at me, puzzled. I hope to God I have not got it wrong and I am supposed to be working today – I've arranged all week around it. I then discover George's puzzled look was to do with the new Hints of Nature tint I tried out on my hair this morning. The trouble is, my hair has been dyed so many different shades of auburn brown in a desperate attempt to find a hair dye that I am not allergic to, the auburn brown is slowly turning aubergine and resisting all attempts to appear natural. Maybe it's time to stop flouting nature and grow in my own colour. But I don't really want to be grey before I'm forty, if it can possibly be avoided.

'How's Luke?' asks George.

I ignore him.

'Not phoned then?'

'How's Norma?'

George launches into a long story about Norma, so called after the Wine Bar he runs. There is fortunately a constant supply of amusing anecdotes to keep two unfulfilled booksellers amused for most of the afternoon.

I'm surprised to see Simon come in, but pleased to note he looks sheepish, so I take full advantage.

'How's Sadie's new job?' I ask. 'Sadie's started up her own Career Advisory Service,' I tell George, who already knows the story.

George scuttles into the back office to fetch a cinematography book Simon has ordered.

'You don't have to be like that.'

'Whatever.' I busy myself with an unnecessary task.

'Your hair looks good.'

I'm not sure what he can mean – my hair looks a fright, but I give in and respond to his reconciliatory gesture.

'Come round,' he says.

'OK.'

'Friday?'

I didn't actually believe he meant it.

'I'll call you,' I say.

George appears with the book, offers Simon a generous family discount, receives his cash gratefully and enthusiastically but luckily manages to fall short of flinging his arms around Simon's neck.

Simon goes.

'Your brother is gorgeous,' says George.

'You would think so – he's got a dick, hasn't he?'

George pretends to be offended. I pretend to do some work.

I drive up to Kenwood to meet Kate for a walk on the

Heath. At the slightest hint of sunshine she's on the phone insisting on exercise. I, however, insist on a visit to the bright new café at Parliament Hill as a reward for such labour. She only agrees because we will then have to again cross the Heath to get to our cars, thus walking off the excesses of such indulgences as home-baked blueberry muffins, double-strength double espresso or hot chocolate piled high with whipped cream – not for me, alas; lactose intolerance and homeopathic remedy prevents either hot chocolate or caffeinated coffee, but doesn't stop the fantasy in which such things are possible.

Kate, burdened in body yet lightened in mind by the eight-month-old foetus, struggles towards me. She looks gorgeous. She always was the prettiest of us all, but pregnancy has transformed her into an angel. I ask if she is sure she can manage the walk. Kate, not one to let anything as demanding as hauling around thirty extra pounds interfere with her life, ignores my libellous remark and opts instead for a forty-minute, relentlessly optimistic monologue on the preparations for the impending birth of the most yearned for, most anticipated, most loved, baby ever.

1979
Now we look like *real* drama students

Franny is waiting for me in the cloakroom. We have not seen each other for three weeks. During the Christmas break I have ditched most of my existing wardrobe, bought a pair of Fiorucci drainpipe jeans, a second-hand tuxedo from Flip in Covent Garden, appropriated my dad's old shirts and had my hair cut like Patti Smith. Franny, too, is suitably reinvented as a drama student in a long dark green Indian cotton dress with mirrored bodice and cowboy boots, her hair frizzed and hennaed.

Suddenly the door bursts open and in rushes a blond elf, hair newly shorn and peroxided to within an inch of its life. She looks even prettier. I hate her. She heads straight for one of the cubicles, not stopping to close the door, and proceeds to retch loudly.

'Kate? Are you all right?'

When she reappears her face is drained of any colour; I'm pleased to see that she no longer looks so pretty. She flops onto the bench next to me.

'Oh, Christ,' she says. 'I hope I'm not pregnant.'

1974
I thought not I should ever see
So mean a heart as thine has proved to be

Why can no one else except me ever be on time?

I have been waiting at Hampstead station for twenty-five minutes before Margie and Toby arrive.

During that time I have entertained a thousand happy endings for the as yet unseen Toby and me.

I mean, when your best friend wants to introduce you to her stepbrother, you know what she means.

What she means is she won't have to worry about me dragging her down, holding her back. I will be taken care of.

And what I dream about is being free from the inevitable humiliation of Margie making moves on my boyfriend.

But when I see him I know instantly that our plans are doomed to disappointment, for the tiny, skinny person that she thinks I will like is the least fanciable boy I have ever come across, with his white skin, flaming red hair and searing blue eyes.

In his favour, Toby does have a passing resemblance to the tragic Chatterton who lies dying above my bed. This, however, is not enough. With no knowledge of the matter, I instinctively understand that this is not a boy who goes for girls.

1976
That's a plenty for me

Toby and I spend the best part of a day and a half combing Kensington High Street and the King's Road for outfits that will not disappoint the Pointer Sisters when we attend their concert at the London Palladium.

On the night I am dressed in a dusky green crêpe 1930s evening gown which was evidently made for a short person as it stops mid-calf on me. The rest of it fits so perfectly that this seems intentional and it looks fabulous. I carry a black fringed shawl over my arm and am wearing my precious beige suede Biba court shoes on their very first outing.

Toby wears an old dinner suit complete with satin stripe down the leg. His long narrow feet are forced into black patent pointed lace-ups.

'50p Oxfam!' he tells anyone who admires them.

This is Toby's birthday treat. I have contributed to part of his ticket. He is not thrilled with this arrangement, but I couldn't think of anything else. Toby is notoriously difficult to buy presents for.

Hanging around outside the theatre, a taxi pulls up in front of us.

I jump backwards, as it had been raining earlier and the roads are still a little wet. Normally I love this as it allows a perfect reflection of the city's lights, but tonight I fear for my shoes.

To my surprise, out of the taxi steps Adam Levy dressed in a white tuxedo (not quite as dashing as Bryan Ferry on the cover of 'Another Time, Another Place'). Behind Adam is the gorgeous Julian, who turns back to the taxi and holds out his hand. A long, thin, beautifully manicured and well-jewelled hand is placed in Julian's and out steps the darkly tragic figure of their mother. I think a hat and veil are inappropriate dress for a concert, but I can't take my eyes off her.

Adam sees me and becomes even more distracted than usual. He looks over at Toby.

'Hi, Adam,' I say. 'You remember Toby don't you? Margie's stepbrother.'

'Oh, yes,' he says. 'Right. How are you?' He holds out his hand to Toby. Toby is a bit confused. No one ever offers to shake his hand. But he takes it.

Adam looks to his mother, who is evidently intrigued.

'This is my mother,' he says, only to me.

'This is Hattie,' he tells his mother.

She moves towards me. I am only one step away from her, but even this tiny space takes for ever for her to cross. She holds out her hand to me.

'Helena Levy,' she says.

I mutter feebly: 'Nice to meet you.'

But she holds tightly onto my hand and appears to be looking me over. Her face behind the veil is over-made-up. Everything about Helena is overdone.

'Hattie. Yes. I've heard all about Hattie.'

Her eyes ooze the bitter acid of disappointment.

I look at Adam, who looks anywhere but at me.

'Enjoy the show,' she says, then turns away. They slowly make their way into the theatre, Julian holding onto her in case she falls, as her muscleless legs have difficulty supporting her fatless body. Adam trails behind.

'What was that?' asks Toby.

A cold shiver sneaks down my spine.

'Let's go in,' I say.

1971

Would you have a minx as your best friend?

The blond girl with the round blue eyes is waiting for me in the cloakroom.

'I've saved you a peg,' she says.

'Oh, thanks.'

'I'm Margie.'

'Hattie.'

'I saw you at the interview.'

How could I forget?

'I'm glad we're in the same class.'

Is she? Why?

I feel awkward in her presence. But I stay with her because now I know somebody.

In the classroom she grabs adjoining desks.

'Sit next to me.'

'OK. Thanks.'

'That boy's staring at you.'

I turn around to see who she means. A strange-looking boy with wild green eyes and long black hair is indeed staring at me. I start to giggle, but there is something disturbing in his look that makes me stop. He winks at me. I don't think I like him. I turn back to Margie.

'He's a bit creepy,' she says. 'But don't worry, we'll just keep out of his way.'

I am pathetically grateful for this show of friendship. So I stick with her. It's much easier to allow people to make friends with you than go to the effort of making friends with them.

'Your mum's strict with you, isn't she?' she asks me.

I am so relieved that she has spotted this that I vow to keep her as my best friend for ever.

I fill up with petrol at Tesco's. I love the new machines where you pay at the pump with your credit card. But I spend far too much time trying to put the card in the right way, and end up feeling like I have tried all possible permutations and been rejected each time (a metaphor for my sex life?). Finally I am accepted. The joy is immense and totally out of proportion to the achievement. (My sex life again?) In the car I turn the mile display to 000.0 – I love all those noughts – and drive away with a feeling of renewal, fresh beginnings, optimism. But I'm immediately brought back to reality by the length of the traffic jam along the North Circular.

I begin to worry about the amount of time the chicken pieces stagnating in the boot along with the rest of the week's shopping have before salmonella sets in and causes Margie and Geoff to leave the dinner early suffering from severe stomach cramps. This may not be at all a bad idea. They are both given to heavily criticising my cooking under the guise of friendly advice – 'Have you thought of adding garlic/basil/oregano (flavour) to this?' – and a touch of salmonella poisoning may well prevent them from accepting any more dinner invitations.

I finally arrive home and curse the lack of a welcoming person ready, willing and able at the front door to assist with ten straining Tesco's carriers and help with the tiresome job of unpacking and putting away.

Due to lightening speed in which my mind works, I have great difficulty in finishing any task. Thus the simple act of unpacking the shopping takes approximately forty-five minutes, during which time I open the post, phone Kate, put on some washing, prepare lunch and reapply my lipstick. Finally it seems that everything is in its place; it will however, be several hours before the toilet duck finds its way to the toilet, only, in fact, seconds before the congenitally late and habitually overdressed Margie and the devoted Geoff (the only man I know still to be sporting a 1970s footballer's perm) ring the doorbell in anticipation of an inferior dinner. I try not to disappoint.

I always feel partially envious of Margie and Geoff for their joint interest that consumes so much of their time together and partially aggravated that they cannot see what has happened to them, that is, that they are bordering on the socially unacceptable in their search for the ultimate taste experience. So I therefore try desperately hard to keep the subject away from 'Ready, Steady, Cook', which chef has moved to which new restaurant or Rick Stein's latest marketing coup in his attempt to take over the planet. Needless to say, I fail miserably.

'Now, I want you to meet our bridge teacher,' says Margie.

'You're learning bridge? How old are you?'

'Actually it's enormous fun,' says Margie. 'You should try it.'

'Yeah, right,' I say.

'Well, if you don't want to meet any new people . . .'

'There is Luke—'

'Oh, Luke – the invisible boyfriend.'

'Actually, I prefer to call him my lover.'

'Of course you do. A boyfriend is someone who wants to meet your friends.'

'Did I tell you I managed to get a table at the Oxo Tower for the twenty-fifth?' Geoff says to Margie, expertly diverting away from a potential minefield.

'Oh, that's marvellous,' drools Margie, experiencing the closest she's come to an orgasm since the last time they went to the Oxo Tower. She turns to me. 'Have you been?' she asks.

I look at her directly in the face, challenging her to really see me.

'No,' I say, 'I haven't.'

'Oh, it's wonderful. And when you book it's worth waiting a couple of weeks for a table by the window. The view is spectacular.'

She and Geoff launch into a detailed analysis of the menu while I distractedly start the washing-up.

Chapter Two

In which our heroine worries about what is going on inside her head, attends a funeral and plans a holiday

My mind is racing at an even more alarming pace than usual, so even fewer tasks are getting completed. I think of the cupboard at the top of the stairs, which when opened pours out cascades of unfinished tapestries. I am living in a complete delusion that one day at least one of them will get finished.

I feel like that woman in the Dorothy Parker story 'The Telephone Call' – the one which goes, 'Please God, don't let me ring him.'

I ring Kate, whose advice is if I ever feel like I want to ring Luke, I must ring her instead. I tell her that this may be an ongoing thing and exactly how many telephone calls is she prepared to tolerate?

If anyone knew what was really going on inside my head, would they still want to know me? The thing is most of my friends do know – that must be a good sign then.

Then I worry that I'm a completely pathetic emotional wreck masquerading as a normal functioning human being. I don't know any men who suffer similar anguish and torment. Or if they do, they're not telling. Perhaps it's due to the fact that, as I read in a recent report, high levels of testosterone impair the ability to articulate. The Research Department could have saved millions by simply going to see a Sylvester Stallone movie. That would have told them everything they needed to know.

I feel the need to destroy something, hopefully not my potential relationship, so I go into the garden to attack the dead wood daring to clutter up the winter landscape. The weather is fortunately mild enough to allow this. I try out my new secateurs, a Christmas present from Sadie, which are crap until I turn them the other way around and then they work perfectly.

This helps a bit. But I still want to phone Luke.

So I phone Kate.

'Do you think I should phone him? It's not too Glen Close, is it?'

'When did you last speak to him?'

'Sunday.'

'It's Tuesday.'

'Is that good or bad?'

'So, what you are saying is, he didn't phone you yesterday.'

'Oh. Yes I suppose so.'

'What's the problem? You'd phone me.'

'I haven't had sex with you. I'm just so out of practice. Is this really what it's like out there? Now I know why I stayed married for so long. Look, is it all right to phone him, or not?'

'If you want to phone him, phone him.'

'But before you said . . .'

'That was because I thought you thought, for some reason, that you shouldn't.'

Maybe Kate is the wrong person to ask for advice as she never has played the rules of the dating game. But then neither has she ever had a one-night stand. Maybe she is the right person after all.

'Oh. OK.'

My mind is no clearer, but I decide to set myself a totally unrealistic target in order to allow Luke plenty of time to phone me before I phone him well before my self-appointed time, which I know I will.

1994
Sometimes Sadie can be such a cow

'This guy was just gorgeous.' Sadie is only half listening; she is attempting to force feed Hannah with a chip.

'Can you believe that there is a child on the planet that won't eat chips?'

23

'When we got introduced he took my hand and stared right into my eyes.'

'Oh, right,' says Sadie. 'The old eye lock trick.'

'What the hell, it works.'

'Come on Hannah. Eat a chip for Mummy.'

'Anyway, so later on he came over and asked me what I thought of the show . . .'

'He's not an actor, is he?'

'Yes, but you know me. Put me in a room full of men and you can guarantee the one I'm attracted to will be the actor. He was knocking back the wine though.'

'Oh, come on, Hattie, you don't need that. Not the boozy actor, please.'

'And then out of nowhere, because we were talking about something else, he says, "I think you are one of the most beautiful women I have ever seen"—'

'How drunk was he?' asks Sadie.

1988
Introducing 'The Colonial'

Dad is concerned about Sadie not being 'one of us'. This never bothered him when Simon and Kate were together. But he must sense that this time it's different. It's not as if religion is vital to our lives; it just gives us a shared sense of suffering, an excuse for feeling victimised and a justification for worrying. It has also given Dad an unhealthy obsession with the Middle East. So his mild protest is more to do with a latent sense of duty than his own real feelings on the matter. But I inform him that, with a name like Sadie, at least everyone will think she's Jewish, even if she's not.

Dad has to be ordered, before the meeting, to refrain from referring to Sadie as 'The Colonial'. He thinks this is highly amusing and refuses to acknowledge the sensitive relationship between us and those who were once part of the Empire.

Dad thinks the West End of London is the centre of the Universe and scathingly refers to anything beyond a one-mile radius of Marble Arch as 'the suburbs'. The further you go from the centre of the Universe, the less intelligent, cultured and human you become.

So Australians don't stand a chance.

'How are things in the Colonies?' is the first question he asks Sadie.

1992
Goodbye Harry

It is not a large crowd; it's mostly made up of a handful of ancient bodies with just enough energy left in them to bid a fond farewell to a fellow traveller.

Franny and I are the only representatives of our generation. I am shocked by this and upset for Franny that no one else bothered to come.

Franny stands at the front, towering above the bent over and shrivelled inmates of the retirement home, now with one available, highly sought after room, due to the recent departure of Franny's father.

Harry lies in a box awaiting his final journey. Although I have always desired cremation for my own used-up body when the time arrives, I cannot rid my head of the image of a journey into flames and its significance. I find this worrying as I have for most of my life been immune to the effects of religious symbolism. I shock myself by willing forgiveness for Harry for choosing this particular method of travel into the next world.

I realise that this is merely because he was the sweetest, kindest, gentlest man I ever met. So how come he has such a crazy daughter?

1982
Oh, Franny! Not again

I am woken up by the sound of the doorbell. The clock says 9.15, so I decide I must have dreamed it. I am not getting up at 9.15 on a Sunday morning for anyone.

The doorbell rings again. Then the knocker knocks. Then I hear a voice through the letterbox.

'Wake up, you lazy cow. I need to use your phone.'

I get up.

I open the door.

'Hi, Franny,' I groan, resignedly.

'I need to phone Fabrizio.'

'What, now?'

She doesn't answer but pushes past me into the living room and reaches for the phone.

'My phone's out of order,' she says.

'Did you pay the bill?'

'You don't mind, do you?'

I look at Franny, her hair redder and wilder than ever. She looks terrible.

'Have you been to bed?'

'Not to sleep.'

I go to the kitchen to make tea, then suddenly remember that Fabrizio has returned home. She is phoning him in Italy.

I go back to the living room to find Franny curled up foetally on the floor, hugging the phone and smiling. She is uncontrollably happy. She laughs and giggles whilst, at my expense, Fabrizio tells her all the things she needs to hear to wipe away the guilt of her infidelities.

I have two favourite Sunday fantasies. They both involve croissants, freshly squeezed orange juice, Sunday papers and 'The Archers'.

Fantasy number one stars me, by myself and loving it.

Fantasy number two stars me and Kevin Kline.

In the Sunday papers (indulging fantasy number one), I read about a game doing the rounds of Hollywood involving how many steps it takes almost anyone you can think of in the history of the movies, to connect to that unlikeable piggy-faced actor Kevin Bacon. Apparently, no one is more than six steps away from him, giving full weight to the six degrees of separation theory which constantly comforts my fantasies. Kevin Kline, who although I know is happily and devotedly married, is only three degrees of separation from myself – Kate once did a play with an actor who was in one of KK's films. This gives an alarming sense of possibility to my fantasy, even though he is obviously seriously happily married. Then I read an interview with Kevin Kline in

27

which he talks incessantly about the happiness of his marriage.

I'm obviously frighteningly in tune with the *Zeitgeist* and wonder why I am not some Julie Burchill-type figure being witty and clever about post post-modern life, instead of an unsuccessful person of undefined career, waiting for the phone to ring so that the person masquerading as my agent can send me to some remote part of the country to perform in a training film that only a handful of trainee insurance salesmen will ever see.

I am standing in Margie and Geoff's unbelievable designer kitchen to end all designer kitchens, trying not to look bored as some boring man explains the process of patenting a new something or other that will bring renewed quality of life to thousands of people suffering from something or other. I shift weight onto my left foot and feel a familiar twinge in my lower back. Grateful for this opportunity of release from the boring man, I excuse myself and try to find a chair high enough to ease myself gently onto without inflicting any further damage.

The party continues around me. I have been sitting, quietly rocking, as advised by my osteopath, on a high dining chair for five minutes when Geoff discovers me.

'What are you doing here?' he asks.

'It's my back. I just needed to sit down.'

'What have you been up to?' he asks.

I ignore his pathetic attempt at suggestiveness.

Thank God I don't have to rely on Geoff and Margie's attempts to provide me with a sex life.

∞

'I hope you don't mind, but I gave your phone number to Geoff's cousin John.'

'Oh,' I say. 'Who?'

'John. His name is John.'

'Anything else I should know about him?' I ask Margie.

'Probably best if I don't tell you anything.'

My suspicions are already aroused.

'How old is he? What does he do? Is he single, separated, divorced? Has he got kids? Where does he live? Why does he want to phone me? What have you told him about me?' I could go on, but Margie stops me.

'He's forty; he sells insurance; he's divorced with a thirteen-year-old son; he lives in Hendon. He, now how's this for a coincidence, he saw you in a training film and I told him that you were—'

'Oh my God, I can't believe it! Not the Insurance film?' But this is not what is bothering me. I feel grateful for Margie's efforts in matchmaking, but she never seems to get it right. Almost everything she has so far told me about John has left me feeling that I do not want this person to even know I exist.

Later that evening Margie rings again.

'Listen, I'm really sorry. But I just spoke to John and he went out with this woman last night and they had a great time, and he doesn't want to see anyone else, so he won't be ringing you. I'm really sorry.'

'That's OK. Thanks for thinking of me.'

I feel mildly put out and strangely concerned that he can know from just one night how he feels, but also pleased that he is the sort of man who doesn't feel the need to keep his options open, then put out again that I have missed this chance. Then I forget all about him.

A week later I am cooking for Kate when the phone rings.

'Hello.'

'Is that Hattie?'

'Yes.'

'This is John. Geoff's cousin.'

'Oh, yes.'

'Margie told you, did she, that I was going to ring?'

I hate his voice. It has that sad, nerdy quality. I know I don't want this to continue.

'I'm sorry,' I say. 'This isn't a good time. I've got a friend here and we're just eating. Why don't I take your phone number and call you back? It won't be tonight, but in the next couple of days.'

I write down the number, say goodbye and return to Kate, making sounds like I've just been touched by something horrible that I need to rid myself of. Well, at least I've given myself a couple of days to decide whether I will ring him.

The next night he rings again and wants to meet for a drink at the weekend. I tell him I am busy, feeling very cross at him for not obeying instructions.

Over the next week he rings incessantly; I put him

off each time. By the following Saturday, I am forced to leave my answerphone on to screen calls. He rings fourteen times, but only leaves two messages. By Monday I realise I have to say something to him to stop this happening.

By the time the phone has rung for the fourth time on Monday, I pluck up the courage to answer it.

'Hi, it's John,' he says cheerily. 'I phoned you at the weekend but you were away.'

How dare he make assumptions about how I spend my weekend? Actually, in yet another of the disturbingly recurring synchronicities in my life, I went to see *The Cable Guy*.

'No, I was here,' I tell him, hoping he feels silly that I know how many times he has rung.

'Can you come out tonight?' he asks, unperturbed.

'Look, John. I'm sorry. I don't know what Margie has told you, but I'm not ready to do this. I thought I was, but I'm not. So, I'm sorry.'

'Hey, no pressure. Just friends going for a drink.' He sounds rational, but I have already been witness to his obsessive behaviour.

'No, no. I'm sorry.'

'OK,' he says. 'It's a shame. I saw you in that film, you know.'

That film!

'Yes, Margie said. I'm sorry. Bye.'

'Bye,' he says.

A week later he rings again.

'Hi, it's John.'

I have so completely forgotten about him that it takes a few seconds to register.

'Last time we spoke you were a bit depressed. I wondered if you were feeling any better and wanted to meet for a drink and talk about it?'

I cannot believe this.

'No,' I say. 'No, no, no. I don't want to come for a drink. I'm not depressed. I don't need to explain myself to you. I don't know you.'

Then he says, 'Look, can I just say something here?'

'No.' I say. 'You can't. Goodbye.'

I put the phone down. I start to laugh because I remember the film; the film that demonstrated how to break through resistance, hook your customer and clinch your deal. Poor John. He wasn't asking me out, he was selling me insurance.

1982
When will I see you again?

We are at the airport, just Franny and me. Typically for Franny, she is weighed down by an enormous carpet bag, several layers of clothing, the ever-present hat, one large, bulging suitcase and small squishy thing for hand luggage.

We are mostly silent. I walk with her to the Alitalia desk to check in her luggage. All our movements are slow in order to stretch out the time left before we have to say goodbye.

We try not to make this parting too dramatic. If her previous luck with men is anything to go by, she will be back among us, her spirit uncrushed, ready to take on the world within days. I hope for her sake this time will be different.

We have deliberately not left enough time for a drink or a shop, so I follow Franny, carrying her bag, to passport control.

'I'd better go,' she says. Her voice is quiet and sad.

'Hey,' I say. 'This is good. Fabrizio is the best thing that's ever happened to you, remember?'

'Look after Harry, won't you?' she says.

'You know I will,' I say. 'I'm mad about him. If I get my way, we'll be married by Christmas.'

Franny smiles then gives me a hug. She takes the bag from me, opens it and takes out a one-eyed, balding bear and hands it to me.

'I want you to take Whitby,' she says.

'But—'

I can't finish the sentence; Whitby goes everywhere with Franny. Without another word, she goes. Once through the security gate, she turns to wave. I wave back, then wave Whitby's paw. She tries to smile, turns and walks away. I stand watching her till she disappears, then clutch Whitby to me and wonder when I will see her again.

1976
Simon's just jealous

'I think you're crazy,' says Simon. 'And I can't believe Mum and Dad are letting you go.'

'It'll be fun.'

'You and Margie and Toby alone in an apartment?'

'Margie's parents will be in the flat next door with their friends. And I am sixteen, you know.'

'It doesn't bear thinking about,' says Simon. 'Margie and all those Italian waiters.'

'I'm looking forward to it,' I say.

'Well, I still can't believe you're being allowed to go,' says Simon.

1976
Margie gets right to the point

'You know what I think?' says Margie. She is twiddling with the straw of her strawberry milkshake.

'What do you think?'

'You know what you should do?'

'No.'

There is a silence before she makes her historic pronouncement. I wait patiently.

'What?'

'I think,' says Margie slowly and surely, attempting to give authority to her opinion, 'I think you should go to bed with someone.'

'What?' I spill chocolate milkshake all over the table. 'Who?'

'I don't know. Anyone. I just think it's something you should do.'

'Why?'

'Because you're the type to have lovers.'

'What are you talking about?'

'How many boys have you been out with?' she asks, already knowing the answer.

'Well, there's Adam Levy.'

'Oh, he doesn't count.'

'How can he not count? He's the first boy I kissed. He asks me out all the time. I've been out with him.'

'He doesn't count because everyone knows that Adam Levy is in love with you. He's so weird about it.'

'So, not him then?'

'God no! I mean, a man.'

'Oh. And where do you think I might find someone to go to bed with?'

'In Italy.'

Up until now, I thought Margie was just being Margie. But she is serious about this.

'Look at you,' she says.

'What about me?'

I know what she means. She means I don't look like her.

'Well, I don't look like you.'

But Margie is genuinely concerned for me.

'You've got to have some kind of experience with men and if they don't want to go out with you, which they obviously don't, then maybe you should just sleep with them.'

I have to admit she has a point. But I prefer to change the subject.

'Lucky, lucky you. No more school. I've still got two more exams.'

'And two more years,' grins Margie.

'Yeah, thanks for the reminder.'

1990
She just doesn't get it

'I'm sorry, but it's always bugged me.'

'What has?'

'Well, if you knew that if you came in contact with water, it *would destroy you, you wouldn't have any water around, would you? I mean you wouldn't just have a bucket of water lying around on your castle battlements.'*

'She's not the only one who lives in the castle,' says Sadie.

'That's right,' I tell Simon. 'There's those weird monkey things. They'd need water.'

'How do you know?' Simon asks me. 'If it was me – if I were the Wicked Witch of the West and I knew that there was a possibility of water melting me – I would make sure that no one around me needed water either. I would only have things around me that could survive without water.'

Sadie gets up to clear the plates.

'You worry me,' she tells Simon.

'Is that why you married me?' he asks her.

'I may have thought twice about it if I knew you had the thought processes of a dictator.'

Simon laughs. Sadie leaves the room.

'She just doesn't get it about the movies, does she?' I say.

'No,' says Simon fondly. 'She doesn't.'

I feel encouraged whenever I make Luke laugh. I somehow believe that being a stand-up comedian makes him an authority on humour. I realise that this is unfair pressure as there are loads of extremely unfunny stand-up comedians who I'm sure would make me feel like an ignorant, racist pig if I ever made one of them laugh.

I'm pleased to hear, though, he has incorporated into his act my spotting the resemblance of a Rovers Return extra to Salman Rushdie.

I've also entered his act as persona of 'girlfriend'. However, I'm not so pleased that 'girlfriend' is used as a butt of misogynist jokes relating to men's inability to comprehend the complexities of the menstrual cycle. Luke spends much time attempting to convince me the joke is on men, not women. I'm not convinced. Especially when I hear myself described as a gremlin.

I tell him, however difficult it must be for him to have me turn into a gremlin every month, imagine what it feels like from my side.

I'm alarmed to hear this comment used in his act, along with the acting out of a sweet cuddly thing morphing into some vile creature, saying lines like, 'Oh, no, what is happening to me?' and get the biggest laugh of the evening. From men, of course.

Chapter Three

In which our heroine discovers the hazards of sharing a flat with your brother and best friend, runs over a dog, learns some distressing news about her brother's marriage and celebrates the birth of a baby

As my mind is so active during the day, I allow it complete rest in the evenings. Once I'm settled on the sofa, I prefer not to have to get up for anything until I decide it's time for bed. But I do like a cup of calming tea after supper and as there is no one here to offer to make me one, I resentfully leave the comfort of Habitat's softest soft furnishings and go to the kitchen to turn on the kettle. As I'm here, I may as well do the washing-up whilst the kettle is boiling, then I won't have to do it later when I'm feeling sleepy instead of just tired.

I return to the sofa – the Sleepy-Time herbal tea bag brewing in my mug, and remember I have to phone Grace to arrange a date to attend Toby's show. I try hard to remember the last time Grace phoned me. I can't. I try to remember the last time I saw her; it was in that advert for a painkiller, all glammed up, filmed in a pastel haze. It's always a shock to see her out of her denim and leather uniform. I remember thinking at the time, 'She looks like a normal person. You'd never know that she is devil bitch from hell.'

I decide, none the less, to ring her.

The phone is answered by the long-suffering Jan. I contemplate the incongruity of Grace doing anything as conventional as committing to a long-term relationship. I ask Jan how her art therapy course is going, then get passed over to Grace.

'Hiya,' she says, sounding ridiculously pleased to hear from me.

'How are you?'

'Really well. We went to Toby's show last night.'

I feel that familiar wash of pain, rejection and abandonment, but I manage to respond with a feeble, 'But I thought . . .'

But Grace is off detailing the sweat and spit count of Toby's performance, a game that has constantly kept us alert in even the most dire of theatrical experiences we've been obliged to endure in the name of friendship.

'When are you going?' Grace tactlessly asks.

I mutter something about not knowing yet and end

the phone call wondering why I continue to call Grace a friend.

1979
She's leaving home

'*And how much are you being asked to pay for this slum?*'

'*£160 a month.*'

'*There are some sharks in this business.*'

'*Not you, of course.*'

'*Hattie, you know your father would never rent out a flat in this condition.*'

'*It's a disgrace. There's mould all over the bathroom wall. God knows how old that cooker is. Those gas fires look pretty ropey to me.*'

'*And look at the stair carpet,*' adds Mother.

The stair carpet is made up from what looks like patchwork pieces which were probably once from a sample book. It's an interesting effect.

'*I think it's an interesting effect.*'

'*Well, at least it's got a stair carpet,*' concedes Dad.

We climb the stairs, red, orange, green, tweed, flower, blue, check, orange, until we get to the next floor. The room I have allocated for myself is bright and sunny.

'*Look at the state of that lino.*'

'*This room might look all right in the sunlight, but it will be very cold in winter.*'

'*It will be fine,*' I say, beginning to get irritated.

'*You've got two outside walls and a flat roof. No insulation anywhere. It will be very difficult to heat this room.*'

'I take it you have nothing nice to say about this flat at all.'

'No,' says Mother. 'It's awful.'

'£160 between three of you, that's £53 per month.'

'£13 a week.'

'I'm not happy about you living here. But I know it's something you need to do.'

I could hug Dad.

'But I'd feel happier if Simon were here with you.'

'What?' I had never considered living with Simon. I was moving away from home.

'He leaves Sussex in June and I don't suppose he'll want to move back home.'

'Of course he will,' says Mother.

'I'll suggest to him he moves in with you. It's not as if he's got any plans, or a job to go to. And it will reduce your rent to £10 a week each. You'll lose a living room, though.'

'I'll have to talk to Grace and Kate about it.'

I am not thrilled with this plan. I don't feel I want a big brother watching over me.

'Simon can have that room next to yours,' says Mother.

Oh, why can't she shut up?

'I think someone should talk to Simon about it,' I say.

'It's probably got rats, this place,' Dad says, poking around the skirting board.

1979
The 'Rat' Incident

Grace is lying on her stomach in a cubicle in the Casualty Department of Whittington Hospital. It is two o'clock in the morning. I am standing on one side of the bed, desperately trying to stifle laughter whilst a nurse stands on the other, sewing stitches into the deep gash in Grace's right buttock.

'Why wouldn't you go to the toilet?' asks the nurse.

I lose the battle with my self-control.

'It's not funny,' says Grace.

I am immediately deadpan, deathly serious.

'Who's laughing?'

'You wouldn't think it was funny if you were lying here. Ouch!'

'Grace thinks she saw a rat,' I tell the nurse.

'Nasty. Try and keep still, please.'

'And she was too frightened to leave the bedroom.'

'I did see a rat.'

'Lucky you had that chamber pot,' I say. 'Pity it couldn't take your weight. Maybe you're not supposed to sit on them.'

'What else are you supposed to do? Fuck, that hurts.'

'I don't know. Perch. Crouch.'

Even the nurse is laughing now.

'Oh, shut up,' says Grace.

1979

How would you feel if it was your brother and your best friend?

'I've got something to tell you,' whispers Kate.

She does pick her moments. We are lying flat on our backs on the floor during our morning exercise class, legs outstretched and hovering three inches above the ground. We must count to twenty.

The strain on my stomach is so fierce I can barely breathe; I don't know how Kate can talk.

I let my legs drop to the floor.

'That was a quick twenty, Hattie,' says Jackie, our dance teacher. 'Come on, legs up high, drop them slowly, now stop. One, two, three, four—'

Jackie should have been in the SS.

Kate's news is going to have to wait.

But not that long.

In the changing room she says, 'After you went to bed last night—'

'Yes?'

'Ummm—'

'What? What happened?'

'Well, Simon and I—'

'Oh my God.' I sit down on the bench, arms in a jumper that has yet to make it over my head. I'm not sure what to think about this. Neither Simon nor Kate are ones for casual sex. So why did I not see this coming?

'You kept all this quiet.'

'It's been brewing for a while. We've been getting on really well. He's a very nice person. He may be one of the good ones.'

'This sounds like serious talk.'

Kate suddenly gets cross.

'Oh, what's your problem? Simon's had girlfriends before.'

'I don't have a problem. I don't have a problem at all,' I say, grabbing my things and walking out.

'And sometimes,' Hannah is telling me, 'when I wake

up in the night from a bad dream I go into Mummy's bed.'

'That's a good thing to do,' I tell her. 'Do you have lots of bad dreams?'

I hand her a badly cut-out petal to stick on her tissue paper flower.

'Sometimes,' she says.

'What do you dream about?'

'Witches and monsters and burglars taking all my toys.'

'Wow,' I say. 'Anxiety dreams at five years old.'

'And sometimes when I've had a bad dream I go to Daddy's bed.'

I stop what I am doing.

'What do you mean, Daddy's bed? Daddy and Mummy sleep in the same bed.'

'No they don't,' says Hannah, then shows me little pieces of pink tissue paper stuck to the ends of her fingers.

'Where does Daddy sleep?' I ask her, hoping she can't detect the panic in my voice.

'In the spare room – where Onya used to sleep when she lived with us to look after me when Rufus was born. I don't want to do this anymore.' Hannah shakes her fingers, attempting to shed the tiny scraps of pink tissue paper that have stuck to them.

'All right,' I say. 'How about *The Sound of Music* and I'll show you the bit where you can see Julie Andrews' knickers?'

'Yeah,' squeals Hannah, running over to fetch the video.

I sit back in the chair. If it's possible, my heart is

beating faster than my mind is racing.

'Come on,' says Hannah.

If I manage to do a minimum of two adverts a year, provided they have European play, or if I'm very lucky, which I was once, worldwide, then I can generally survive most of the year with the part-time job at the bookshop, signing on for brief periods and doing the odd stint at any one of the large exhibitions – helping hang pictures for one or two of the smaller galleries at Art Live, selling herbal teas, incense and crystals at the Mind, Body and Spirit Exhibition or demonstrating some new kitchen gadget at the Ideal Home.

My life has been like this for so long now that I no longer even consider the fact that I am waiting for the big break, the part of a lifetime that will propel my life into a different stratosphere where I suddenly become a contented, settled person, with no money worries and oodles of friends who all just want to be near me in case any of my talent and luck rubs off on them.

I think I know now, because I saw it happen to Kate, that a few good parts and a degree of public recognition won't change your life; it won't change the things you believe in, the things you want, or the people you love.

All it means is that you've done a few good parts and got a degree of public recognition, that's all.

So when Luke suggests to me that I ought to have a go at stand-up, I don't immediately go into the 'most-successful-female-comedian-since-Victoria-Wood' fantasy.

Well, not immediately.

I hear the excessively noisy sound of the post being deposited through the letterbox. I always expect that the noise should produce far more post than ever actually arrives. Today's offerings are no exception; a solo envelope lies halfway down the hall. I imagine a scenario in which the local postmen hold a contest to see if any of them can get the mail to land on the mat. So far, none of them has succeeded.

I recognise, before picking it up, the size and shape of correspondence from my solicitor. I momentarily forget that I'm in the throes of applying for a mortgage and the stress of divorce resurfaces. I open the letter in a Pavlovian response of dreaded anticipation, only to find a request for information required to secure the loan. I breathe a huge sigh of relief and retire to my bedroom in an attempt to accommodate the unwanted feelings of rage that the reminder of my marriage always unearths.

1985
A pleasant surprise

Adam rings me quite out of the blue. It must be four or five years since I heard from him. He's been travelling, he tells me. He'd like to get together, take me out for dinner. I'm impressed. No one offers to take me out for dinner. I pick up that he's had some kind of drug problem. I'm not surprised to hear this – Adam was always a little

displaced. But he keeps telling me that he's better now. He tells me
he is working with his brother in the family jewellery business. He
has a flat. He sounds settled, normal. He'd always been troubled
and I've had my fill of troubled men, but now he's better, he says,
and I believe him. I agree to meet him for dinner, mostly just because
he asked me. And because he's not an actor.

1989
Escape from The Acid Queen

Adam and Julian are seated at one side of the rattaned, coired, tropi-
cally decorated conservatory. Adam is smoking and murmuring,
for ever uncomfortable in his brother's presence. I am perched
on the edge of a wicker armchair. Helena sits opposite me, as
over-groomed as ever. Helena isn't actually sitting. She never
really sits. It's something between sitting and languishing. Some
sort of yoga position, perhaps. She seems to contort herself into
a deliberately uncomfortable pose so that any movement out of
it appears to be an enormous effort. Everything in Helena's life
appears to be an enormous effort. She picks up a small bell from the
table next to her, and dangles it. You would have to have exceptional
hearing powers to recognise this sound as the summoning of a bell,
but an obviously well-trained, dainty Filipino house maid enters.

'Thank you, Lily,' Helena says to her. 'You can serve tea now.
Hattie, did you want a peppermint tea?'

I decline, feeling that this would be too much effort.

'Thank you, Lily.'

Lily is allowed to leave.

'I spoke to your mother.'

'Oh, yes,' I say.

'She said that everything is under control and it's all going very well.' She pauses. I hate that pause. But Helena's speech groans under the weight of pauses.

'I have to say that I, well, both of us,' she slightly turns her head towards her eldest son, including him with one tiny movement that Adam would sell his soul for, 'we are a little concerned that everything will be all right.'

Now I get it.

'I'm sure it will be,' I say.

'I don't want you to think that I'm interfering—' Helena repeats Helena's favourite refrain.

'Then don't,' I say.

Helena was not prepared for that.

Julian comes to her rescue. I hate the way he does that, but Helena burdened him with responsibility as soon as she was abandoned, shortly before Adam was born. Julian got the responsibility; Adam got the blame. Julian is only two years older. Two years and a lifetime apart.

'Now, the Goldwins,' he says, 'that was a wedding.'

Five hundred people at the Grosvenor Rooms; three months later the seventeen year old bride was back home with her mother.

'We could have a wedding like that, if that's what you want,' I say. 'We could also have a marriage like that.'

Helena is confused. She is not used to being challenged. Most people are too frightened of upsetting the balance of her already delicately balanced nerves. She looks to Julian, but he is looking at me as if he's never seen me before.

'There were many reasons why that marriage didn't work,' says Helena. To say she is jumping to the defence of her friends gives the wrong impression, for Helena would never do anything as energetic as jump. 'But I don't think anyone could say that the wedding was one of them.'

Adam is giving me a 'please-don't-do-this' look. I ignore him. He has been warned.

'Oh, really,' I say. 'Well, I for one wouldn't be at all surprised. If those children had to put up with a fraction of the shit that Adam and I have had to, then they were bound to be at a disadvantage. And how dare you suggest that my parents aren't capable of making a decent wedding for their daughter. They'll do it their way and if it's not good enough for you, then don't come, because I won't miss you.'

Outside I am shaking.

'That went well,' says Adam.

1985
I'll never forget that night ...

As we cross the lights at Camden Road, I suddenly see it walk calmly in front of the car.

'There's a dog,' I scream at Adam.

Too late. We've hit it.

Adam pulls over.

'What should we do?'

Adam is already out of the car.

I follow him. The dog is lying, severely wounded, in the middle of the road.

'Do you think we should move it?'

Adam is not quite sure what to do.

'Move it,' I tell him.

He drags the dog to the edge of the road. By now it is convulsing badly.

'Has it got a collar?' I ask.

'What?'

'A collar. Maybe it lives round here. We should tell whoever owns it what we've done.'

' "What we've done",' repeats Adam. 'A dog walks in front of my car and gets run over. What have we done?'

'We've killed it,' I say.

The dog is now lying still.

1989
Spoilt bitch

I have the usual mile-high, guilt-wrapped pile of birthday presents from Adam. These include a Nicole Farhi silk dress, shoes, bag, earrings, antique silver perfume bottle and a bottle of Chanel 19.

But I cry. Because what I really wanted, what I really thought I was going to get, was a puppy.

1982
Dad gets it wrong

Over the usual overcooked, dried, tasteless roast chicken, Mother has produced for Sunday lunch, Dad makes an announcement. He has been waiting patiently for Mother to finish her review of the week, which amounted to a litany of visits to various medical practitioners in a desperate search to find something wrong with her.

'I've got a surprise for you, Simon.'

'Oh, yes.'

'It's, er, well, I got it from, it's only borrowed, you understand—'

Dad is unsure whether to tell the story or tell the surprise. Simon waits patiently.

'Yes? So? And?' I say.

Dad gives in.

'It's a pirate video copy of ET,' he says proudly.

'What?' I say. 'But the film's not even out yet. Where on earth would you get a pirate copy of ET from?'

Stupid me, I've given him the platform to tell the story he wanted to tell all along.

Simon and I are not impressed.

'I don't want to watch it,' I say.

Dad's face falls.

Simon glares at me.

'The whole point is going to a cinema,' I say, irritated by my father's ignorance. 'Having the experience. Seeing it on the big screen.'

Dad looks at Simon.

'Sorry, Dad.' *His tone is kind and sincere.*

'I've got it for the weekend, if you change your mind,' *Dad says.*

'We won't,' I snap.

Simon kicks me under the table. He is always doing that.

1987
Two Days in Tahiti

'The only clue you're getting is that it's a film,' says Toby.

'OK,' I say. 'Do it again.'

'I went on holiday for two days in Tahiti.'

'That's it?' asks Kate. 'That's all we have to go on?'

'*Two days in Tahiti. What the fuck does that mean?*' asks Grace.

'*Do another one.*'

'*All right,*' says Toby. '*This is a singer. I went on holiday to Paris and Rome for three days then Nice and Cannes for two days.*'

'*You're spelling something out,*' says Adam.

I look at him, shocked.

'*How did you know that?*'

'*I've played this game before,*' he says.

'*When?*' I can't imagine when he could mean.

'*The trick is,*' says Adam authoritatively, '*not to spell out what it is. Spell out clues instead. Then it takes longer to guess.*'

'*Why do we need longer to guess?*' asks Grace, handing me a joint. She always does that, even though she knows that I'm just going to hand it straight on. That really pisses me off.

'*I give up,*' I say. I have no patience with games I don't understand.

'*I think I've got it,*' says Kate. She goes and whispers to Toby, who smiles and nods. '*I'm going to do one.*'

'*Go on then.*'

'*Right,*' says Kate. '*I went on holiday for three days to Morocco. Then Peru and Romania for two days, Greece and Nova Scotia for one day then New York and Thailand.*'

I feel the colour drain from my face.

'*Pretty bloody weird holiday,*' says Grace.

'*My God,*' I say. '*Does Simon know?*'

I'm just thinking that Kate should receive an award for the longest recorded pregnancy for any mammal that is

53

not an elephant, when the phone rings. It is Mike, sperm provider to the most shrivelled foetus, with the news that the male population of Kentish Town has just increased by one. Kate is doing this alone, but I'm pleased she at least allowed Mike to be present at the birth.

I'm thrilled to bits, especially to hear that the tortuous procedure of erecting the birthing pool in the spare bedroom and filling it with warm water every twenty-four hours for the last fortnight, finally paid off and Kate got the birth she wanted.

I immediately dash to John Lewis baby department, then spend far too much time choosing a completely useless soft toy, knitted booties, Babygro and a cute woollen hat.

While I am at the shops and the sales are still on, perhaps I should just have a quick look around. The morning's post had brought a bank statement with the news that last month's standing order payment on my new bed was the last. I misguidedly convince myself that this means I now have an extra £132 to spend each month and, as I haven't treated myself to new clothes for weeks, I could now afford maybe one thing in the Nicole Farhi sale.

Naturally I find an absolutely can't-live-without black polo neck, only £80, something my wardrobe has been clearly lacking in for years. I also see a quite perfect grey and black cardigan at the ridiculously reduced price of £120.

I work out that I could buy both if I put half the amount on my Visa card, which may just have enough room on it.

I go to the till with my fingers crossed, desperately

hoping to be spared the humiliation of a rejected Visa. I am accepted. Hurrah! I hand over my Connect card to make up the balance, believing that I have actually only spent £100 and leave the shop proudly bearing my Nicole Farhi carrier. Almost better than sex.

At home I discover that the second post has brought a Visa bill demanding the instant minimum payment of £100.

Damn. Foiled again.

Chapter Four

In which our heroine tries to have a baby but acquires a puppy, loses her virginity, joins a bookbinding course and discovers the secret to the perfect relationship

Sadie is living under the delusion that her little talk has had some effect. I have suddenly become the perfect aunt, picking up Hannah from school, offering to take Rufus to Tumble Tots and generally behaving like a responsible, caring person.

What is actually going on is I am working hard to secure Hannah's trust to get as much information out of her as possible on the state of her parents' marriage, as neither Simon nor Sadie has given one hint behind the reason for separate sleeping arrangements, despite tentative enquiries on my part.

I worry about how Dad will cope with the news that neither child has been able to sustain a lifetime relationship. Mother will just identify with The Queen and thereby improve her standing at the Ladies' Guild. It will also give her much sympathy and therefore attention. Mother will not mind at all.

Hannah, however, is not so eager to talk about her home life. In fact, the more time I spend with her, the less she tells me. I feel I have wasted too much time and money on trips to McDonald's, the toy shop, Saturday morning film club and Spice Girls paraphernalia for no return.

An unexpected byproduct is that Sadie is enormously grateful and lightens up on me. She even begins to take an interest in my latest passion – bookbinding.

'What can I be funny about?' I ask Luke.

'Wrong question,' he says. He has his back to me and is rifling through my utensil drawer, searching for the bottle opener. It is lying on the work surface next to the fridge. I hand it to him. He smiles his crooked smile that hides his crooked teeth.

'But I can't think of anything.'

'You're trying too hard.'

I've spent the whole day watching endless videos of endless comedians whilst attempting to make notes on things like observational humour versus character based; length of gags; timing; running gags; use of catchphrases; one-liners; counting laughs. I've come to the conclusion that everything and nothing is funny. All sources have been drained dry. I'm not even going to attempt to do this.

'This is wrong for me. I won't be able to do this.'

'I think you'd be making a mistake.'

Luke makes me laugh sometimes.

'Why do you think I should?'

'Because you're funny. And you're always performing.'

'It's in the writing not the performing. There's a big difference between being naturally funny and writing funny. I've never written a thing in my life.'

'It's in both. All these people get up on-stage and create a persona, a character that is a comedian. You can do that, you're an actress for God's sake.'

'Why do you think I can?'

'I have total belief that you will be able to do this,' says my lover.

1971
But look at all those people

I am standing at the school gates. The playground looks vast. It is vast. Two football pitches, four netball courts vast. And there are hundreds and hundreds of children all dressed like me in brand new royal-blue blazers.

My mother is standing with me.

I cannot quite bring myself to enter the gates.

If only I knew somebody.

It is all too much. I burst into tears.

'My daughter felt like that,' the woman my mother is talking to says, 'but she didn't do it.'

1982
Visiting Harry

Harry is showing off the latest postcard from Italy. 'Do you think she's happy?' he asks me.

I smile and nod.

Sometimes it's easier to answer with facial expressions than endure the tiresome process of responding and then repeating louder and louder to the ultimate frustration of us both.

A middle-aged woman steers a tiny old lady in a wheelchair past us. Harry waves the postcard in her face.

'My daughter,' he shouts at the figure in the chair.

'Eh?' says the old lady.

'My daughter,' shouts Harry even louder. 'She's in Italy.'

'Eh?' says the old lady. Her daughter wheels her on.

'Nice old girl,' says Harry, 'but she's deaf as a post.'

'Poor thing,' I say.

'What's that?' says Harry.

1990
Sometimes lying is all right

I've just spent all day helping Toby white-wash his roof terrace. As we painted, we performed every Pointer Sisters' routine we could remember, so the job took quite a while. Walking home, my shoulders are burning and my arms and head are aching.

I am not in a good mood.

Adam's car is parked outside the flat.

He could not have possibly got to Brighton and back in this time, plus spent a decent amount of time with Julian, Melanie and the kids.

Something must be wrong.

I run into the flat.

I call out.

'I'm in the garden,' he replies.

I run into the garden. Our garden is built into a steep hill. There are steps up to the lawn area and at the top of the steps, staring me in the eye, are two black beads and a pointed nose.

'What the hell is that?' I say, laughing to hold back the tears.

'It's Harvey,' says Adam.

1991
The things you have to do

This is the third day running I've had to do this. With an uncomfortably full bladder I lie on a bed, have cold gel smeared on my abdomen, then a sensor run over it. The nurse gets a clear image on the screen of my ovary, then measures the size of the eggs it has recently expelled. If they are declared healthy enough, I then get dressed and walk two blocks down Harley Street to another consulting room, where I undress again and lie on another bed to have Adam's healthy, newly washed sperm injected into my womb.

Everything has been carefully calculated for optimum success.

I have been taking and plotting my temperature for weeks. Adam has been wearing boxer shorts and using cold flannels.

Sometimes you have to give nature a helping hand.

Sometimes nature declines the offer.

The two best investments I've ever made are a box of five thousand staples for £1.50 and a roll of two hundred perforated sheets of clingfilm for £1.69.

Despite fairly consistent use, neither is showing the slightest sign of running out.

Hannah has a desperate urge for a strawberry jam sandwich. I'm out of strawberry jam and bread, but Hannah is 'desperate', as she keeps informing me in an increasingly whiny voice.

Eventually I give in and agree to a trip to the shops to buy jam and bread.

The local Italian deli has a fine range of jams and honeys, so we head there. Searching the shelf for strawberry flavour, I find every other berry plus kiwi, fig and mango. Funny, I always thought mango was strictly the preserve of chutney.

I wonder if Hannah would notice if the sandwich was on Ciabatta bread and spread with Little Scarlet jam instead. I fear she would, so we leave the lovely deli and head for Budgen's.

Naturally I come out with more than I went in for and, as I am struggling with the carrier bags Hannah says, 'I'm seeing Daddy on Saturday. He's taking me swimming.'

I drop all the carriers.

1991
And your test for today is . . .

Standing in the kitchen cutting up chicken for Harvey, I suddenly burst into tears.

The chicken leg is broken.

'Oh, God,' I think, 'the poor chicken.'

And I have this horrible image of battery chickens crammed into cages, squashed against each other so tightly that the pressure breaks their bones.

I may have just seen Schindler's List.

I vow then and there that if chickens have to live like this, it won't be because Harvey wants to eat one. I shall put him on a dried food diet immediately.

Adam arrives home and the phone rings, both at the same time.

He picks up the phone.

'It's Sadie,' he tells me.

'I'm pregnant,' she screams down the phone.

The tears will not stop, but somehow I manage to hide this from Sadie and make, I hope, suitably thrilled noises and show enough interest for her not to guess the level of pain I am in.

I spend the rest of the evening locked in the bathroom, huddled on my crying chair.

Adam doesn't come anywhere near me all night.

'Your good points,' I say.

'Witty, charming, intelligent, talented, creative, loving, caring, sharing,' says Franny.

'Tell me someone who isn't going to describe themselves like that to a total stranger,' I say.

'What should I leave out?' she asks.

I laugh.

'OK, now faults.'

Franny thinks for a long time.

'Well I don't want to scare anybody off. What do you think I should say?'

'The attention span of a goldfish, incapable of throwing anything away and never puts the tops back on jars properly.'

'Don't I?'

'You know you don't.'

'What else should I say?'

'Oh, Franny it's you whose answering the ad, not me. What do you want him to know about you?'

'That I'm desperate for a shag?'

'That might be exactly what he wants to know. Come on, that's not all you want.'

'No. Oh, God, why am I doing this?'

'Because it's a perfectly valid way of reaching out for the like-minded people that it's so hard to connect with in this disparate society we live in.'

'Then why aren't you doing it?' asks Franny.

'I'm not that disparate,' I say.

'I heard this joke today,' Luke tells me.

'That must be tough.'

'What?'

'Well, doesn't it get a bit boring? I mean, just because you're a comedian people think they have to make you laugh.'

'That's what you think. You told me.'

'And you told me I did make you laugh.'

'You do.'

These conversations that go nowhere depress me. They feel like an omen.

'So, what was the joke?'

'There's this God-fearing, law-abiding man who's caught in a flood. He refuses help from his neighbours saying, "God will provide."'

'The rains continue, the waters rise and a rescue boat arrives. He refuses to get in the boat saying, "God will provide."'

'The rain gets worse and the waters rise even more.'

So now he's isolated on the roof of his house and a helicopter arrives and lets down a ladder. He refuses to get into the helicopter, saying,

"God will provide."

'He drowns. When he gets to Heaven and meets God, he says,

"All my life I have worshipped you and lived by your laws. Where were you when I needed you?"

'So God said,

"I sent you a boat and a helicopter, what more did you want?"'

'That's not a joke,' I say. 'That's a warning.'

1976
An omen?

Half way through The Omen *I start to get a panic attack. Nausea, flushes, shakes. It is so bad I have to leave the cinema. Adam is very good about it. He puts me in a taxi and sends me home.*

1968
Queen Anne's legs

There's this game we play in the car. Simon looks out of his side window and I look out of mine and we score points on the amount

of legs in the name of any pubs we pass. But if you get the name
of a tree, you lose all your points.

'Pig and Whistle,' shouts Simon. 'Four.'

'Two.'

'Since when did pigs have two legs?'

'Look at the sign. The pig is standing on his hind legs. So
two points.'

'No. That's not how we play. It's in the name. Pig and Whistle.
Pig has four legs. I get four points.'

Simon sits back, gloating. I cross my arms and my face.

'Pub coming up on the right,' says Dad.

Great, my side.

'Ha! The Queen's Arms. No points,' says Simon.

'Two points,' I say.

'It's called The Queen's Arms not The Queen's Legs. No
points.'

'That's not fair. Dad?'

'Well, it could be Queen Anne,' says Dad.

'So?' I say.

'She had very famous legs.'

'What?'

'Don't you know anything?' says Simon. 'Dad's always going
on about Queen Anne legs. Our dining chairs have got them.
Haven't they?'

'That's right,' says Dad.

'Goody, then I get twenty-six points.'

'How do you work that one out?'

'Four for each dining chair, six fours are twenty-four. And two
for the pub.'

'You can't do that. You can't suddenly count chair legs as points.
You're such a cheat. You can't bear it just because you're losing.'

I scowl again.

Mother turns round to look at me.

'Don't make faces, please.'

'The wind will change,' says Dad.

'It already has,' says Simon.

1976
That holiday

Margie and I have the same outfit. This is unheard of. Her mother takes her to far more expensive shops than my mother takes me. But I tell my mother which shop I want to go to for holiday clothes – Bus Stop in Kensington Church Street. And she agrees.

She buys me the most gorgeous royal-blue cotton, fifties-style, zip up the back shorts and halter-neck top with matching, full-circle, buttons down the front skirt. The halter-neck top is edged with a blue-and-white striped frill, as are the side pockets of the skirt. I am mad about this outfit. I think it is the nicest outfit I have ever been bought. And it is so unlike Mother to buy me something I like.

But Margie has it too.

I no longer like it so much. I mean, you can seriously go off something if you see it looking better on someone else. Margie fills it out more. She has more curves than me. A straight line has more curves than me.

But now Margie has cottoned onto the fact that she looks better in my clothes than I do, so for most of the holiday she wears my clothes.

I only brought two bikinis, but she is always wearing one of them. She wears my dressing-gown in the mornings, my swimwear on the beach and my dresses in the evening. And if we go on a sightseeing trip or shopping, which is what the Bus Stop outfit is perfect for, she wears hers so that I can't wear mine.

They like Margie in Italy. She looks so different from Italian girls. And the Italian boys won't leave Margie alone; not Mario or Silvio or Paulo or Gianni.

I lie around in the shade reading Death in Venice; *Toby attempts to soak up the sun, following it across the sky until it sets, flat out all day long, and Margie teases the local boys, letting them buy her drinks and ice creams and occasionally rewarding them for their devotion with a peck on the cheek. Never anything more.*

Only one of them is curious about me. Bernado. He is not the same as the others; he's more cocksure, pleased with himself, precociously sexual. Out of all the boys, he's probably the only one with any real experience and he knows there's no chance with Margie because he knows her type. But me. I'm something else. I'm different.

He comes and sits by me. He's clever; he knows how to play the game. He asks about my book. He asks about me. He talks little about himself. But what do I need to know?

He is older. He has his own apartment. He invites Margie and me and Toby and some of the boys round to his place. He gives us wine and plays his guitar. Then Toby and a couple of the boys decide to go dancing. Margie and I stay. Bernado puts a record on.

Margie and Silvio start to dance.

Bernado gets up and holds out his hand to me. I take it and he leads me into the bedroom.

And then, as Joe Cocker growls his way through 'A Little Help From My Friends', I am slowly and painfully fucked.

Bernado was wrong about Margie.

❈

I have gone to bed early. Too much sun or something has left me drained. I need to sleep.

I become aware of Margie's mother in the room.

'Where's Margie?' she asks.

'I don't know,' I say, half-asleep.

Toby is shaking me awake.

'Where's Margie?'

'I don't know.'

Margie is sitting on the edge of my bed.

'Where have you been?' I ask.

'I'm not a virgin anymore,' she tells me, then starts to cry.

❈

There's two things I can't remember about me and Adam. The first time we had sex. And the last time we had sex.

1994
Hello stranger (1)

To keep out of the way of the removal men, I stay in the front room where the bookshelves are. All the boxes labelled 'Books' come in here and I begin to unpack them and put the books on the shelves.

Now and again I step out to check on the progress of the enormous amount of things that seem to be coming off the van.

Going back to the front room, I see one of the men – young, interesting-looking, with a soft Northern Irish accent, looking through my books. I like him. I find him very attractive and I love his voice. But what can I say?

'Are you interested in books? What do you like to read? Would you like to go out for a drink? Would you like to go to bed with me?'

But I say nothing. I just smile. He smiles back then leaves the room and continues his work.

'What the fuck is going on?'

'I'm fine thanks. How are you?'

'Where are you living?'

'Oh.'

'Yes, "Oh".'

'Who told you?'

'Who told me? I can't believe this. Your marriage is breaking up and you don't tell me – you don't even tell me that you've moved out. I have to find out from Hannah. Why didn't you tell me? I can't believe you didn't tell me.'

'Because I knew you'd be like this.'

'Like what?'

'Make it about you.'

'What do you mean?'

'Look. I'm really busy at the moment.'

'When can I speak to you?'

'I'll phone you tonight.'
'From where?'
'Speak to you later.'
He puts the phone down.

It never matters how many people there are. It could be half a dozen in a small room above a pub or three thousand in a cavernous auditorium. I've done them both. And it always feels the same.

I love the way smiling and clapping go hand in hand, as it were. It's quite hard to clap without smiling. It's a happy action. It's about sharing good feelings. It's like saying, 'You did this for me, now I'm going to do this for you. You made me feel good. Now I'm going to make you feel good.'

And as you look out into those smiling faces you feel the most appreciated, the most acknowledged, the most accepted, the most believed, the most trusted, the most enjoyed you will ever ever feel.

And this, you believe, is the only place where that can happen.

And that is mostly why I do it.

1993
Looking through the Wedding Pictures

I look ridiculous. The look I've gone for is Ethel Merman in the final scene of There's No Business Like Show Business. *Tight-fitting white lace, long tight sleeves, then it flounces out from the knee in yards of white net that trail behind like a fish tail. It's a kind of mermaid look, I suppose, or should I say Merman.*

Can't imagine why I ever thought Ethel Merman was a good look to go for.

1993
Throwing away the Wedding Pictures

It is a totally empty gesture. But I do it anyway, attempting to give it symbolic significance.

But before I tear them all up and throw them away, I look through them.

I don't know who most of these people are. What were they doing there?

1993
I've got something to tell you

We are in the kitchen.

Mother is making sandwiches. Although I saw her take the smoked salmon out of the fridge, I know it will taste lukewarm when I eat it. The usual soggy, limp excuse for a salad is already on the table. Dad is watching the lunchtime news.

I know I have to tell them. That's what I came round to do. Deep breath, here goes.

'I've got something to tell you.'

Mother stops and looks up. She's already got it wrong. Oh, God, she thinks I'm going to tell her I'm pregnant. Why else would she have that inane grin on her face?

'Adam and I are separating.'

That got rid of the grin.

'Why?' *she asks immediately.*

As if I'm going to tell her.

'We don't want to be together anymore,' *I think is the most noncommittal response I can make.*

'But, why?' *she asks again.*

So I tell her.

'You know when you mistake something for something else, it takes on the characteristics of what you believe it is? And the more you look at it, the more it becomes what it isn't. And when you finally see it for what it really is, the qualities it had that you'd anyway only imagined are nowhere to be seen.'

I look at Mother directly in the eye.

'I don't know what you're talking about,' *she says.*

I look over at Dad.

'Well, I can hardly say I'm surprised,' *he says.*

'What? Why? What do you mean?'

'I'm sorry. He's a nice boy. But he's not for you.'

This is news to me. Dad has been nothing but charming to Adam ever since he's known him.

'I always knew that temper of yours would be your downfall. You always were highly strung. I'm amazed he stood it as long as he did.'

'Well, you know where I get it from.' *I throw a look in Mother's direction. Mother responds with her standard hurt, quivering lip look.*

I am shocked that he can dismiss this so lightly and I am hurt that he automatically puts the blame on me.

But if that's what they want to believe, I haven't got the energy or the desire to tell them what was really going on.

I don't think their little lives could take it.

Luke is away a lot. This inevitably creates an imbalance in the relationship and makes me feel like he has all the control; it feels like he is fitting me into his life instead of the other way around. I would love to be able to have the opportunity to fit him into my life; but instead I have to settle for brief liaisons in between Luke's heavy touring schedule.

Naturally I worry about 'life on the road' and the opportunities for meaningless sex that it offers. I know, I've done it. But I also know that Luke is not the type for one-night stands. I know because he told me. Also I can tell because of how he is about it. Sex, that is. No. I can almost believe that a one-night stand for Luke would be totally out of character. Now I can't work out whether this is reassuring or not.

I get so used to Luke not being around that when he is, it takes a while to remember that he is someone that I see and not just an absent figure that I think about along with Michael Maloney and Kevin Kline.

Besides, I have plenty to occupy myself, what with the occasional casting session and, of course, my new passion – bookbinding.

I'm convinced that everybody else on the bookbinding course is much better at it than me. I feel a little concerned about the prevalence of animal skins used in this particular craft and try to think of designs that preclude the use of anything that once gambolled over a mountainside.

I have two weeks to decide on the subject for my end of term project. I'm the only one not settled on a choice of book. I don't want to be too obvious and choose an Angela Carter novel as this would not feel like a challenge. No – I need something that will stir the soul.

Wild-eyed Carl, who dresses in combat gear and exists in a parallel universe, has picked *The Satanic Verses*. Can just imagine. Pretentious, loud-voiced Jessica has picked *Ulysses*, but I think she just wants us to believe she's read it, and ultra-glossed lipstick lesbian Lissa has gone for *The Bell Jar*.

I would love to do *Waterland* with real water. Or *The Turn of the Screw* with a free screwdriver? *One Flew Over the Cuckoo's Nest* in bird shit? I must take this seriously, but my mind has gone blank. Inspiration is not coming from anywhere and everyone around me is too preoccupied to assist; Luke with his career, Kate with Baby Bardolph (I can't believe she's called him that), Franny with her mission to find a man for whom she is perfect, Margie with family, food and the new edition of *The Good Restaurant Guide* and Simon and Sadie with the break-up of their marriage.

I'll just have to sit and wait for a flash of inspiration. This might be a good time to begin meditation.

Simon finally calls me.

It is a difficult conversation.

'Kate had the baby at last,' I tell him by way of a warm-up.

'Yes,' he answers.

'I wasn't sure if you knew.'

'Yes,' is all he'll say.

He won't give too much away. He won't tell me where he's staying. And he asks me not to tell Sadie that I know.

'But this is crazy,' I tell him. 'What happens when I'm round there and it's about the time you come home from work and I say "I'll stay to see Simon"?'

'Well you won't say that because you'll know that I won't be there.'

'But won't Sadie think it's odd if I don't say that?'

Simon is getting cross.

'These are minor details. All I'm asking is that you say nothing, then we can play the whole thing down and hopefully things will be back to normal soon.'

'She threw you out, didn't she?'

Simon doesn't respond.

'And there's me thinking you're shacked up with some little editorial assistant you've met at work – which is why you wouldn't tell me where you were staying.'

'What goes on in your head?'

'You know, editorial assistants – they're always anorexic twenty-three-year-olds with great hair cuts and dressed all in black from Agnès B. Men love all that. I'm constantly jealous of them. Them and television researchers.'

I hear a baby crying in the background.

I try to think which of Simon's friends may have a small baby.

Then I hear Kate's voice.

1988
Kate's big break

Kate is so excited and talking so fast that I can barely distinguish her words.

'Slow down. I can't understand what you're saying. But I take it it's good news.'

'I got the part. I got it.'

'Wow. That's amazing.'

'Why? Didn't you think I would?'

'Of course. I mean I hoped you would. But you were up against all those American actresses as well. I'm thrilled for you, but I'm just amazed.'

It's always like this. We can be thrilled for each other, but there is always a little part of all of us that will be wild with jealousy. And this is the most important job that so far any of us have been up for, let alone got.

'I'm going to know someone in a movie,' I sing. 'This is so exciting. When do you go? Where do you go? How much are they paying you? Oh, my God.'

'Don't know. New York. Don't know.'

'New York! I'll come over. Adam and I will come to New York while you're there. God, it'll be such fun.'

'It's not that big a part,' says Kate, suddenly playing it down.

But it always goes like this.

1988
I LOVE New York!

Last time we came, we stayed at The Mayflower. We liked it there.

For different reasons. I loved the view over the park. You have to ask for a room above the eighth floor so you can see over the trees. And Adam liked the hotel's reputation as a place where the music business stayed. It meant there was activity at all times of the night and there was a vague chance of sharing the lift with an 'almost famous but can't quite place the name guitarist' from a 'haven't quite yet made it to the top' group. I mean, if you were really famous you wouldn't stay at The Mayflower, you'd have your own apartment like Eric Clapton, who we walked past crossing at Madison and 61st. The Mayflower had just the right amount of sleaze for Adam. At least it wasn't The Chelsea.

But this time we want to try somewhere different. So we book into The Paramount. Ultra-trendy. And right in the centre. It tries hard not to look like a hotel. So you enter the gloomy lobby and peer around for the reception area. Once located, you can check in, then a bellboy with a long ponytail, dressed in a black suit with white T-shirt, called Dominic, takes your luggage and leads you to the lifts. The lifts are tiny and lit by red bulbs. More gloom.

Dominic opens the door of the room. All we can see is a bed and two other doors. The bed takes up so much of the room that Dominic, Adam and I cannot all fit into it at once. There is a long thin narrow window that looks out onto other long thin narrow windows. The television is high on a bracket on the wall. One door houses a small hanging space. The other is the bathroom. Well, it has a toilet, a shower and one of those weird conical stainless steel wash basins.

I hate this place.

Dominic leaves us.

'I hate this place.'

'It's not that bad.'

'Look out of the window. I want to see New York.'

I eventually manage to convince Adam of my deep unhappiness. So we ring The Mayflower and they can give us a room. Tomorrow.

I don't sleep at all that night.

I spend most of it watching the television. I love American television.

But my best moment is, while channel hopping I come across Woody Allen's Manhattan.

Perfect. Except for the lousy hotel room.

1988
A good idea gone bad

I insist on a visit to the Erté Gallery and buy two prints from his alphabet. An A and an H. Back in London, I have them framed. But the framers put the letters the other way around; so above our bed, in a black mount and gilded frame, sit the letters H A.

HA! Some joke.

Toby doesn't put so much pressure on Margie as he does the rest of us. As long as she presents her face at whatever show he's in, sits through an unspeakable meal (and this is some feat for her) as he performs his After-Dinner Cabaret and faithfully watches for his fleeting television appearances, generally Toby leaves her alone.

Toby has not got on with either of Margie's husbands. Neither have I, for that matter.

❈

Dad suggests *Memoirs of a Dutiful Daughter*. I'm not amused.

Mother has not got one sensible suggestion. Not even a funny one. But Dad begins to enjoy the game and, much to Mother's increasing infuriation, we keep it going for quite some time.

'*If This is a Man.*'

'I could use a picture of Toby.'

'*The Age of Innocence.*'

'Wrap it in a nappy.'

'*The Great Gatsby.*'

'Ooh, white linen, lovely.'

I can't remember the last time I left their house having had a good time.

❈

'But don't you see? It's perfect!'

I am in shock. I can't believe even this of Franny.

'But what about them? Don't they mind?'

'Phil's got another girlfriend.'

'Oh, my God. It gets worse!'

'But she lives in LA so he doesn't see her very often.'

'So what's the deal? Are you seeing Greg, and you and Phil are each other's bit on the side? Or are you seeing Phil, and Miss LA and Greg are the bits on the side? And do you do it with both of them at the same time? What?'

'They're only physically identical,' says Franny, as if that would explain it.

'I'm sorry, I don't understand. Do they do this a lot? It's very weird.'

'I'm trying to explain it to you if you'll listen.'

'Go on then.'

'They are only physically identical—'

'Yes, you said that.'

'What I mean is, in every other way they are totally different. They dress differently, have different jobs, like different things, live different lives.'

'Except they both fancy you.'

'And that is what's so odd. It's never happened to them before.'

'And why do you think this is OK?'

'Because neither of them is perfect. Like Greg has never seen *It's a Wonderful Life*.'

'You said you could never go out with anyone who hadn't seen *It's a Wonderful Life*.'

'Right. But Phil has and he loves it. But Phil isn't remotely creative. He works in the city.'

'You couldn't be with anyone who isn't creative.'

'I know. But Greg is. He makes these amazing stained-glass mobiles. They're just gorgeous. And Phil earns lots of money so can take me to really nice places. He wears the most gorgeous clothes. And Greg is always broke, so either we go to the pub or stay in. But I wouldn't want to do either all the time. And because they are so different, I'm different with each of them.

It's like they both have a girlfriend except it's the same person.'

'So who's better in bed?'

'They're both completely different.'

'So if you fancy a long slow, tender, loving sharing fuck you ring Phil. And if you want a bit of rough play, an intense but fully satisfying quickie, you ring Greg.'

'Well, actually it's the other way around.'

'Franny! I wasn't being remotely serious. You should be able to get it all from the same person.'

'But I don't, do I? And I never have. Have you? That's why it's perfect. I'm physically attracted to both of them; I mean, I love the way they look and I love lots of things about both of them. With both of them in my life, I should be able to be fully satisfied on every count.'

Her logic is unimpeachable.

'And when you say they are identical, do you mean – identical—?'

It doesn't seem to matter how much I try to expose Hannah to the finer cultural delights, she will always be much happier in front of a BBC video, preferably starring the educationally subnormal postman from a fictional Yorkshire village inhabited by strangely accented folk who seem to take for ever to get even the simplest of tasks completed. It can sometimes take a whole episode to retrieve a lost hat from the river or fix the broken village pump. The pace of life is far too slow for me. Happy Greendale residents could all benefit from a rocket up the arse, or maybe a bomb should be dropped on the village and put all of us out of our misery.

I upset Hannah enormously by singing along with her to the theme tune, but using my own lyrics that aptly describe what I think of PP and his fucking cat.

But the one that I really cannot tolerate is that horrid, spoilt, greedy Noddy and his pimp, Big Ears.

Mother banned Enid Blyton in our house, so Simon and I grew up oblivious to the delights of Toyland or even the adventures of the Famous Five, Secret Seven or Nauseous Nine or whoever they were. And now I can actually see why.

Toyland is a microcosm of a Reactionary Society in which the work ethic is to the fore for very little personal reward, thus creating frustration in the work force and an inferior quality of work. Take the story in which the pimp sends his worker out in the rain to ferry Toyland residents around, supplying him with only an old broken umbrella. Noddy has an accident, blames it on the umbrella and has his car, his only means of support, confiscated.

I'm also concerned about the story in which Pink Cat loses her tail and Martha Monkey finds it and wears it as a scarf.

'Fancy wearing it as a scarf,' says Noddy with obvious envy in his voice.

The next scene reveals Noddy, having retrieved the stolen item from Martha Monkey, with said tail draped elegantly around his neck. Noddy as a cross-dresser?

Clockwork Mouse is a hideous kind of juvenile delinquent; the Skittle family are figures of fun to be continuously knocked over.

'The Skittles simply love being knocked over,' we are told again and again.

Did anyone ask the Skittles?

And as for the goblins; they are simply the innocent victims of apartheid who are not allowed to drive cars and are thus forced to trick Toyland's only driver into taking them, and ultimately, him for a ride.

But Hannah is addicted to Noddy and her obsession reaches its logical conclusion with a Christmas gift of a replica, life-sized, red and yellow car.

I argue with Simon over this one, who seems to parent with the adage 'If you can't beat them—' (which we all know is strictly illegal) '—just buy into the merchandising instead.'

Chapter Five

In which our heroine gets caught in a tangled web
of deceit, has an encounter in France, attends a
family wedding and forces a change in her relationship

I suddenly become aware of Kate's voice.

'Have you?' she is asking me.

'Michael Maloney has just gone into that café,' I tell her.

'I thought you weren't listening.'

'What should we do?'

'Go in there too?'

I have, in the last eighteen months, after eighteen
years of distant idolising, contrived two opportunities

to meet and speak with the said object of my intense crush. But I'm not prepared for this meeting.

'I can't,' I say.

Kate marches into the café; I have no choice but to follow her.

I go to a round table and sit facing away from the room, but into a large mirror with a panoramic view of the whole room. Michael Maloney is at the counter ordering food.

'I'll get the coffees,' says Kate. 'Anything to eat?'

'I couldn't possibly,' I say, holding my stomach in a futile attempt to settle dervishes.

Kate laughs and goes to the counter.

MM sits at the table behind me. Perfect. He has a copy of the *Independent*, a notebook and a John Irving paperback. I smile and feel reassured in a kismet kind of way, as John Irving used to be my most favourite contemporary American male author. In my brief career as a founder member of the unofficial North London JI Appreciation Society, I wrote him a long letter, phoned him on a radio show and queued for hours at a book-signing.

This reminder worries me.

When Kate returns with the coffees I ask her, 'Do you think I'm obsessive?'

'I just know, you know.'

'I think there may be a lot of reasons why you don't want it to be "the one". Like the one you thought was "the one" turned out not to be.'

Sadie's doing her therapy talk again. Sometimes I just want to be able to have a conversation with her. Tell her what's happening for me.

'So why isn't he?' She takes out her tobacco tin and starts to roll a fag. This always intrigues me. Sadie, Ms-right-on-PC-organic-vegetarian-eco-woman rolls her own, like some old toothless pigeon racer in a flat cap with a pint of stout.

'There's not enough that's on my list.'

'You did a list?'

'Yes, you know like the kids in *Mary Poppins*.'

Sadie gives me that 'movie' look out of the side of her face. I try to recover the moment.

'I wanted to be very clear about what I didn't want. I don't want to fall into the same trap again. This is about moving on, breaking the patterns, learning the lessons. God, if you don't want to learn the lessons, you don't deserve to be here.'

Sadie puts the brown paper in her mouth. She lights it. It sputters. I move away. She smiles.

'So what is it about Luke that doesn't come up to scratch?'

'I don't feel that I'm top of his "Things To Do" list.'

'Oh, he has a list too, does he?' Sadie laughs her awful laugh.

'OK. Fair do's. I mean, he's holding back.'

'So are you.'

'Yes, I know.'

'Isn't that all right?'

'I don't know. It's so exhausting. It's like there's all these rules. The things we're not allowed to talk about. I know what it is. Nothing bothers him. I mean, it must do. But he doesn't tell me. Then I say he's secretive and he says he'll tell me anything I want to know. But I don't know what I don't know, do I?'

Sadie laughs again.

'But the point is, you're out there. You're doing it. It's your first one since Adam. And sometimes it's frustrating and tormenting and you can't make any sense of it and sometimes it's easy and wonderful and everything's all right.'

'Yes,' I say. 'That's exactly how it is.'

Sadie stubs out her tiny cigarette.

'Don't give yourself a hard time. You'll know when it's not right for you anymore. Meanwhile, enjoy it. Of course, if you really want my opinion, I'd have to meet Luke.'

'Yes, I know. That's another big thing, isn't it? Thanks,' I say, not remotely convinced that, even if I came to the conclusion that it wasn't right, I would be able to act on it. It took me years with Adam, after all.

'It's not a "thank you" thing,' she says.

The phone rings.

'Hello.'

'We have to talk.'

Kate is so good at tackling the difficult stuff, but I don't see why I should make this easy for her. Both her and Simon have shut me out.

'Yes. So talk.'

'Can't you come over?'

'Won't that be a bit awkward, what with Simon there and everything?'

'Simon's at work.'

'Of course he is.'

'You're going to make me work hard for this one, aren't you?'

'I know none of this is about me. But it just seems like everyone else is making it about me. All that "Don't tell Hattie" stuff.'

'It's not just you. It's just that you're caught in it from all sides. Simon and Sadie just want to be able to sort out their problems on their own.'

'But they're not, are they? He's involved you, for one.'

'Actually, it was Sadie's idea that Simon came to stay with me.'

'I don't believe that for a minute. You mean she knows and for some reason she doesn't mind?'

'It's what Simon told me.'

'Well, of course he'd tell you that. Hasn't he got any other friends who'd have him? He could have asked me. Kate, I can't believe you agreed to this.'

But I know why she did. Because she will always love Simon. She wants to help him. Be there for him. Sometimes Kate isn't very good at putting herself in the big picture. She thinks of others too much.

But, after all she went through, why shouldn't she want to live out, however briefly and whatever the circumstances that allow it, the fantasy of her and Simon and a baby? I hope she's strong enough for it.

'I forgive you for not telling me,' I say to Kate.

She laughs.

'Come over?'
'See you in a bit.'

1983
The power of sex

I am sitting upstairs on the bus. I don't normally like to do this. But it was unusually crowded downstairs. I couldn't get my usual seat. So I came up here among the smokers. If there's anything worse than the Monday morning bus ride into work, then it is having to endure cigarette fumes. I'll suffer it until Baker Street when the bus empties, then go back downstairs.

Halfway down Lisson Grove, a couple come up the stairs. They are a little older than me, in their mid-twenties perhaps? They are both tall and long limbed. They both wear raincoats. Hers is belted, his is not. They sit in the empty double seat in front of me. They lean heavily against each other.

She has a vague music business look, blond Debbie Harry hair. He looks like a student, cropped hair, round wire glasses. They turn to face each other and touch noses. She turns away. Then she lifts one long arm and, revealing long unpainted nails, she runs her fingers through the back of her hair whilst stretching her neck. He responds by putting his arm around the back of the seat and gently squeezing her shoulder. She lays her head against his.

They sit like this for a while. Not talking, just barely touching. We are way down Regent Street by now and I have completely forgotten about the stink of smoke because the aura of sexual fulfilment that exudes from this couple is completely intoxicating.

I want more of it.

1976
Margie's mistake

After the holiday in Italy, I have another holiday with the parents in France.

Margie sends me a letter. It's in two parts, written over five days.

In the first part she writes of how much she misses Silvio, how much she thinks of him. How she sees his face everywhere – in the streets, on the television. She's desperate. She's in love, but he's in Italy and she's only had one reply to her four letters.

How can she live without him? How can she live with what she's done? What they did. Together. She should never have done it. She gave away something that was too precious. She can't live with herself.

The second part tells of how her mother found and read the first part of the letter and knows everything that happened. Her mother is in despair. Things are not good between them.

But had she ever told me about James? The son of her parents' best friends? He's very nice (he never used to be) and he asked her out and she went and they had a great time and she's so happy to be with an older man who knows what he wants and where he's going.

And by the time I get back from France they are engaged.

I've finally settled on Bruno Bettleheim's *The Uses of Enchantment*. Everyone, including retired hairy hippy, Todd, our tutor, thinks this is a bizarre choice and that I've actually managed to out-pretentious, pretentious

Jessica, who has dropped *Ulysses* and opted for AC's *The Magic Toyshop* instead.

The reasons for my choice are:

a) It's more than a book – it's a blueprint for a way of thinking.

b) I've always been compellingly drawn to explanations of fairytales.

c) I loathe the illustration on my paperback copy.

I would like the book to be hidden in some kind of magic box, meaning, if you are open-minded to this book, you will find it; if you are not, you won't. Also, this would reference the literary and cultural use of boxes from Pandora onwards. I'm very excited by this idea; the trouble is, I will actually have to make the damn thing, which looks all well and good in theory but may prove impossible in practice. Fortunately, I also have to hand in a detailed analysis of the concept.

Todd can't quite bring himself to tell me that what I imagine is unachievable, so I end up having a long argument with him about the reasons for doing the bookbinding course, i.e. wanting to combine physical labour with intellectual challenge. But his point is that I am better at the thinking than the doing.

Yeah. That just about sums it up.

1991
What I hate about the theatre is ...

Toby and I have never worked together before. He has pursued a career in musical theatre. My talents in that direction are not nearly strong enough. I can carry a tune, but lack power and feeling. I can pick up a tap routine, but lack style and grace. I'm too different-looking. I wouldn't blend into a chorus line.

We are doing a fringe production of a new play. It's the standard formula of trap five people who would never normally come across each other in a bar/bus station/broken-down train/waiting room/whatever and see who learns what about themselves and each other.

It's only a so-so play. I am playing a mad, sad poetess (I knew all that Zelda Fitzgerald and Dorothy Parker would come in handy one day) and Toby is playing a troubled, closet homosexual mother's boy, serial killer. Or is he?

There lies the tension in the plot.

After three days of rehearsal, I'm sorry I agreed to do it. The Writer/Producer/Director is an embryonic megalomaniac. To make matters worse, WPD is also playing a small, but vital, role. He is never sure which hat he should be wearing and none of us are ever sure which one he is actually wearing. At the end of the first week I am so uninspired I decide to turn up, speak the lines and try not to fall over.

Toby is furious with me. He says I am sabotaging the production.

I tell him, bollocks to the production.

I am being uncharacteristically unprofessional and get treated to a 'this is the whole problem with the state of fringe theatre' speech from almost everyone I know. If those doing it can't commit themselves to it, then how can we expect anyone else, i.e. audiences, producers, casting agents to bother? And that's what the fringe is there for, so that we can shine in the parts that no one else will give us.

But I'm tired of all that.

I'm still not pregnant and Adam won't talk about it. He won't *talk about the lack of baby, the lack of time he gives us to be together or the lack of love in our relationship.*

When Toby has stopped being cross with me, I tell him why my heart is not in this play.

Then Toby gets even crosser with me. Nothing is more important than what happens out there every night under the lights. He can say that because he has no life outside 'the business'. I can't feel that anymore. I remember the feeling. It was one of the best. I'd like to get it back again. But not here in this dirty room, with these desperate people.

Three days before we open, WPD tells us that unless we achieve advance bookings of seventy-five per cent houses in the next two days, then we cannot open. He didn't allocate sufficient funds to pay the rent on the theatre.

We never open.

Toby enters a deep depression. I feel exonerated.

So Toby and Adam and I go to France together instead.

1991
Car crash in France

We are in a traffic jam, driving, or rather not driving, back to the apartment along the coast road. This may be picturesque, but it is also insane. We are not moving at all. The car behind us, however, does move, but not having anywhere to go, only succeeds in crushing our rear lights.

Toby panics. We tell him to stop squealing. But he is terrified of Helena and worries that he may somehow be held to blame. We are in Helena's car.

The car that went into us is a dirty old Renault, but the man who steps out of it is the kind of Frenchman you only ever see in French films but never in France; well, at least not on the Riviera, which seems to be mostly populated, in the summer anyway, by the inhabitants of North West London.

He is gorgeous, deeply apologetic and quite, quite charming. Definitely the kind of Frenchman you only see in films.

I melt and Toby preens.

'Not to worry,' he tells us, 'I work at ze BMW garage at La Napoule. Ring me and I will fix ze car, no questions.'

He and Adam exchange numbers; he then grins at us in a gorgeous French Movie Star kind of way and gets back in his car.

'He seems nice,' I say, trying to sound normal, my insides churning over.

Adam is oblivious. He is too stressed out over the prospect of explaining this minor accident to his mother.

'It'll be fine. It wasn't your fault,' I say, my brief moment of fantasy crashed to earth, as usual, by Adam's insecurities.

I have just got out of the shower. I go to find Adam, who at this time of the evening is usually sitting on the balcony smoking and reading. Toby is by the pool, catching the last of the evening sun before it disappears, depriving him of ten or so potential, but futile, tanning hours.

Adam is not on the balcony.

He is sitting by the phone. Fuming.

'I don't fucking believe this,' he says.

'What?' I ask. Well, you would, wouldn't you?

'That guy. They've never heard of him at the BMW garage. He doesn't work there at all. Now what am I going to do?'

'That's odd,' I say.

'Odd? It's not odd,' Adam shouts. Adam hardly ever shouts. 'It's a fucking disaster.'

'Have you phoned your mother?'

'Of course not.'

'Suit yourself,' I say. He has become fixated and won't be open to assistance on this one.

The phone rings.

Adam picks it up.

I go to get dressed.

'That was him,' says Adam a few minutes later.

'Well, there you go,' I say.

'He wants me to meet him in an hour at the Martinez to discuss it.'

'Did you ask him why he lied?'

'No, I didn't.'

'So, we can go and meet him and then go to eat, can't we?'

So we do.

Monsieur French Movie Star Liar cannot hide the look of disbelief on his face when he sees me and Toby with Adam. But he is not alone either. He is accompanied by an enormous dark blond, proudly possessed of a fine pair of breasts. She has poured herself into a black, sleeveless, backless catsuit and is balanced dangerously on high black shoes.

'I hope you don't mind,' he says, 'but I have brought my sister.'

I am lying in the sun on the balcony, reading.
Toby is by the pool. Still white.
Adam appears, swinging his car keys.
'I'm just going into town for some batteries,' he says.
'OK.' I go back to my book.

While minding Baby Bardolph as Kate half-heartedly attempts to reflatten her stomach at an aerobics class, I get the first idea for a stand-up comedy routine. While jigging Baby Bardolph in his baby chair with my foot, I write the following:

The Relationship Aerobics:
  One step forward
  Two steps back
  Push away, push away.
  Two steps forward
  One step back
  Push away, push away.
  Tiny steps
  Baby steps
  Bigger steps
  Giant leaps
  Feel that high
  Sink down low
  Push away, pushed away.

I show it to Luke later, who says there are enough female comics doing that anti-man stuff and he thought better of me than to sink to those depths.

I don't think he understood.

So I show it to Franny, who at least recognises a truth in it and, if not laughs, then smiles.

1992
After the funeral

I've just left Franny's. I offered to stay, but she said she was so out of it, it wouldn't make any difference if I was there or not. I don't really like leaving her on her own when she is feeling so alone, but she said she must learn to get used to it. It's not as if her father lived with her. It's not as if there is suddenly space in her home where there wasn't before. She just, now, has nowhere to go on a Sunday.

I tuck her vodka-filled body up in bed, then place an empty bucket by the side for her. And leave.

I turn out of Franny's road onto the dual carriageway. I turn too wide and a car racing down the middle lane clips the front of my car, sending my bumper and number plate spinning across the road. I pull over. The other car pulls over in front of me.

'Shit, shit, shit,' I say, hitting the steering wheel with both hands. I don't get out. It's late, cold, dark and wet. Suddenly there's a face at my window. Then a tap.

I wind down the window.

'That could have been serious,' he says.

He looks like a policeman. Big. Big head, big features, big voice. I don't like him.

We exchange names and numbers and insurance details.

'Are you all right to drive home?' he asks.

'Yes,' I say, suddenly very wary. 'It's not too far.'

'Well, take it slowly.'

'Yes,' I say.

I wait in my car until he gets into his and drives off. Then I drive very slowly home.

A week later he rings me and asks me out for a drink.

I say no thank you, I'm married.

Adam thinks this is the funniest story and repeats it to everyone, for ages.

Adam can have a very cruel sense of humour.

1986
Meeting Maurice

Adam is taking me to meet his father.

Maurice lives near Bognor Regis in your ideal English country cottage. He paints, he cooks, he tends his garden, plays his violin and occasionally submits critiques of inaccessible tomes to journals hardly anyone reads.

Maurice is as adorable, warm and welcoming as Helena is distant, cold and unfriendly.

Helena does not know we are here.

Neither Julian nor Helena know that Adam has developed a relationship with his father. And this has contributed greatly, if not singly, to my reasons for falling in love with Adam. Not his ability to deceive those who love him, but his desire and drive to find something good in his life. And Maurice is a good person.

That day I learn that sometimes people are not what they have done, just who they are.

But later I forget that I knew that.

Simon and Dad very rarely lose their temper. It must be a man thing in the family. The women, i.e. my mother and I, scream at each other if the occasion demands it, but Simon and Dad remain calm, quiet and rational, thus fuelling Dad's confirmed prejudices on the delicate balance of a woman's nerves.

Sadie, neatly illustrating Dad's theory, is also volatile. But of course she would be, because Simon has grown up around volatile women. Those are the women he loves. Naturally Dad also puts her propensity for erupting down to the fact that she was brought up in the Southern Hemisphere. He's crossed the equator, he knows what they're like.

Now Dad is worried about Hannah. Rufus is all right. At under two he is already displaying the male restraint prevalent in the family. I try to point out that Hannah has no more tantrums than the average five-year-old that isn't being allowed her own way and Dad retorts: how come I know so much about children without the benefit of having my own?

Dad and Mother have still been told nothing about Simon and Sadie's separate living arrangements. Simon brings the kids round at the weekend and Sadie's non-appearance is put down to, 'giving her a break'.

Dad accepts this with a conspiratorial wink. We

always spent Saturdays shopping and visiting Granny with Dad so that Mother could regain her strength in order to get through the arduous jobs of the week that she had an au pair and cleaning lady to help her with.

Simon has been warned of Hannah's way of dropping bombshells into the conversation. So he has a reward system in progress. If Hannah gets through an afternoon at Grandma and Grandpa's without mentioning Mummy, she gets that week's *Pingu* magazine. So, whenever Dad or Mother bring up the subject of Sadie, Hannah collapses in fits of giggles, then sits upright with her mouth firmly shut.

Dad and Mother are completely bemused.

Honestly, deceit can be so exhausting.

'Why don't you tell them?'

'It might be all right soon and then we'd have worried them for nothing.'

'It's been a month. Are you and Sadie managing to talk yet?'

'We've been to a couple counsellor.'

'One that Sadie found, I suppose.'

'Yes. So?'

'Don't you find that a little controlling? Perhaps a touch disempowering?'

'It says to me she's making a serious commitment to sorting out our marriage. And where do you get all this bloody psycho-babble talk from, anyway?'

'"I've done my time on the couch."'

'"Well, if a bed isn't handy."'

Simon and I laugh. It seems ages since we've been able to do that.

'How long, seriously, can you stay at Kate's?'

'She's not throwing me out. It's nice. It's been good.'

I don't like what I hope I'm only imagining in his tone.

'Be careful,' I say.

'What's this?'

'What?'

'This "Be careful" stuff?'

'Kate's really vulnerable at the moment—'

'Oh, we're all fucking vulnerable—'

Silence.

Long silence.

'I just meant—'

'OK, point taken.'

'I'm seeing Kate later. Will you be there?'

'At some point.'

'See you then.'

'Yeah.'

1989
The Helena and Maurice problem

Adam would like to be able to ask Maurice to our wedding.

I tell him that, as my parents are paying and therefore in charge of the guest list, there shouldn't be a problem.

But Adam knows that it is impossible for Helena and Maurice ever to be in the same room together.

Not even for weddings or funerals.

Helena has buried herself in a tomb of hatred and bitterness. She wants to show the world what Maurice is capable of. That nice, good, kind man that everyone adores is capable of destruction. He has destroyed her life. She will never let it go. When people look at her, she doesn't want them to see her. Only what Maurice has done to her.

She lives grandly. It was always her family that had the money. And everything must be perfect. At all times. I see this side of her as her fighting spirit, although she would never admit to having one. She entertains regularly and hugely. She parades Maurice's crime around parties, openings, balls. If not alone, then with the only man who is allowed to escort her. Julian. Maurice by proxy.

1972
Why teenagers can't win

'Don't put your elbows on the table.'

'What kind of stupid rule is that?' I ask, my elbows remaining firmly put.

'Do what your mother says.'

'But why?'

'Because I'm your mother, that's why.'

'I didn't mean why that. I meant, what is it about elbows that they shouldn't go on the table?'

'It's bad manners,' says Mother.

'Oh,' I say. 'Those old things.'

'And where do you think you are going to get in life without manners, young lady?' Dad asks.

'If manners is about putting elbows on tables, then I don't want to be wherever it is that they're so important.'

'So you want to go and live with a bunch of savages, do you, running around the place naked?' asks Dad.

'I expect there are a lot of very happy savages who don't give a toss about table manners.'

'You are going to have to curb your tongue,' says Mother.

'Is that bad manners too? To have different views from your parents?'

'Not only is it bad manners, it's one of the Ten Commandments,' says Dad. 'You have heard of the Ten Commandments?'

'So suddenly it suits you to get all religious. You've never bothered about it before.'

'I think you should go to your room,' says Mother.

'Oh, right. So not only do I have to take my elbows off the table, I have to go to my room. And suppose you told me I had to jump off a cliff? I suppose I'd have to do that, too?'

Simon speaks for the first time in ages.

'You always have to take things just that little bit too far, don't you?'

'If you won't listen to us, at least listen to your brother. He's got more common sense in his little finger—'

'And what does that mean? How can you have common sense in your little finger?'

'Hattie!' Dad and Simon chorus. Mother gets up to clear the plates. I get up to go to my room.

'And help your mother clear the table, can't you?'

I give up.

1992
Married life

We have two sofas. One sits along a wall. And the other faces the window, dividing the long room. I lie on the one by the wall, my feet towards the window, facing the television in the corner. Adam sits on the other sofa. If I want to look at him or talk to him, I have to turn my head.

Sometimes I am reading while we watch the TV. Adam is either rolling or smoking a joint.

Harvey lies on the rug in front of the fire.

When it's time for bed, Adam takes Harvey for a walk around the block. I go upstairs, get undressed, wash, get into bed and continue reading.

Adam appears eventually, having got undressed upstairs in his dressing room, gets into bed and turns the television on.

I usually fall asleep first.

It's like this for years.

1988
Now that's what I call a wedding

Julian, of course, has the most perfect wedding. His bride, Melanie, is beautiful, rich, well connected and absolutely right. Unfortunately she is also stupid. I am surprised that Julian has compromised on this quality. He is not stupid at all.

But Melanie has made a lifetime study of 'rightness'. She is dressed by the right designers, she eats in the right restaurants and their two homes, house in Regent's Park and large flat in

Brighton, are furnished by the right Interior Decorators. She knows, if not personally, then by recognition from their photos in the right magazines, all the right people.

As far as Helena is concerned, Melanie is perfect.

Adam and I fall far short of the mark and somebody's concern has reached me in the form of offering to pay up to £500 for a suitable dress for me to wear at Julian and Melanie's wedding. I don't believe this is Adam's generosity, but I say nothing and accept gratefully and do the rounds of the shops and discover that £500 is neither here nor there.

You can spend a lot less and look reasonable but, if you want to look knock-out, £500 doesn't go very far. Not if you have to buy shoes and accessories as well. So I end up buying something black and slinky from Ghost, which isn't cheap, but feels like me and I still have enough for a decent pair of shoes.

Adam is furious with me. He had, however, at no point suggested accompanying me on my shopping trips, so I declare it is just fucking tough if I don't look right enough. You can't give someone money then demand how they spend it. He told me I should have had something made. Why didn't he suggest that at the beginning? No. I'm just supposed to know, because we live together, exactly what he demands of me and our relationship. Well, I can't unless he tells me.

When I start talking like this, Adam cuts off. I get nowhere.

Naturally at the wedding I feel woefully underdressed and out of place. Mainly because I am not carrying a Chanel handbag. I feel totally isolated from Adam and his family, none of whom make any effort to include me. I am in none of the photographs.

I am furious with Adam. It should have been his responsibility to make sure I was included. We have been together for four years.

We have a joint mortgage. Is that not enough of a public declaration of our commitment?

Evidently not.

To make matters worse, the parents are there. But at least Simon is there too. Dad loves every overdone, extravagant, flower-filled, ghastly moment of it. And Mother just smiles a lot. Sadie is not there. Their relationship is not yet established enough for her to be included in the extended family. Lucky her.

Helena spends the evening sitting at her place at the top table receiving compliments and attention and never once getting up. Except for a disgustingly sentimental show of filial devotion when Julian gently steers her around the dance floor. She gets a standing ovation. I feel sick. Luckily Adam misses this display on one of his visits to the gents, which see him returned with manic flashing eyes and a more than usually frequent desire to sniff.

I am past caring.

Adam won't dance with me, so I keep sending him over to aged aunts to give them a thrill. He seems to enjoy doing this. As do the aged aunts.

I dance with Dad.

'Of course we're not in their league,' he tells me.

'What do you mean?' I ask.

'I hope they won't be disappointed at the wedding we provide for you. It can never be on this scale.'

This is out of line.

'There are no plans for a wedding,' I say.

'I'm sorry to hear that. Beautiful girl that Melanie.'

'If you like that sort of thing. She's stupid though.'

'You really must try not to be so scathing and dismissive of people. She could end up as your sister-in-law. Then you'll have to get on with her.'

'Why?'

Dad doesn't reply.

1988
My sister-in-law Melanie

Melanie has two weak features that please me enormously. Thick ankles and short stubby fingers. No. She has more than thick ankles, she has bad legs and splayed feet that force her to walk on the balls, thus giving the impression that she bounces along. It is far from elegant.

Not only has she short stubby fingers, but she bites her nails and the gloriously over-gemmed rings look less than glorious on her weighed down, short, fat hands.

Other than that she's perfect.

It may have been a joy to her that she has married a successful jeweller, but she is no advertisement for the merchandise. I always get a moment of internal glee when I see her. She tries so hard to live an enviable life – her life would not be worth living if there was no one to envy it. I wonder about her friends. Do they spot a kindred spirit with whom they can swap anecdotes about inferior interior designers, Range Rover accessories and the difficulties in obtaining a network for the mobile on the fifth floor of Harvey Nicks? Or do they see her for the dressed-up, jumped-up, vacuous social climber she actually is?

It's no wonder that Melanie has no time for me. Oh, she likes the theatrical gatherings, the minglings with the not-famous-yet-but-might-be-one-day, who make up first-night parties. But I suspect that Melanie senses that I don't fall for all her crap. Her lifestyle does not impress me.

She's never been nasty or cold. Often she goes out of her way

*to attempt to be friends. But Melanie and I can never be friends.
We're on different planets. She doesn't understand me and, God
help me, I haven't a clue about her.*

*The only thing I do understand about Melanie is that there is
no actual Melanie. There is no one there. No essence. No soul.
She is not real. She is like a Christmas decoration that sparkles and
delights, brings momentary pleasure and an illusion of something
beautiful. But it only looks good on a Christmas tree for twelve
days of the year. Let's face it – as an object, it's pretty bloody
useless. And out of situ – it's just plain ridiculous.*

'I'm just completely in love with him,' Kate tells me,
lifting a naked Baby Bardolph high into the air then
rubbing her nose into his belly.

'Who wouldn't be?' I say. 'He's divine.'

'He's just so beautiful,' she says, laying him on his
changing mat.

'Isn't he?' I say, gazing into his smiling eyes.

'I don't need anyone else in the world,' she tells his
adoring face. 'You are everything.'

'That's wonderful,' I say.

We marvel at him in silence for a while as Kate
gets him dressed. She is such a natural mother. Her
movements are swift and confident. She's not afraid of
him. She doesn't treat him as if he's delicate and she
might break him. And she manages everything she used
to do without appearing encumbered or slowed down
by his presence. She's a natural.

'You should have done this years ago.'

I can't believe I said that.

'I'm so sorry. I can't believe I said that.'

Despite Baby Bardolph being slung over her shoulder, Kate comes to me and gives me a hug. That is so Kate. I wound her and she comforts me.

Franny decides it's time she met Luke at about the same time I decide it's time I met Phil, or Greg, or both.

We arrange a date. But there is still much to ponder on. Should we all go out or should one of us cook? If we go out, where should we go? If it's Phil that's coming, then we can go anywhere because he is so generous he'll probably pay for us all. If she opts for Greg, then Franny will end up paying for both of them and do I always expect Luke to pay for me? No I don't, but he usually does. Franny might find that uncomfortable if she's paying for Greg and Luke pays for me. So I suggest it becomes a 'girls taking the boys out' night, but Franny thinks that might intimidate them too much as we are the only ones who know each other.

I could have everyone round to me, but I'm always cooking for Luke so that won't feel like a special evening to me. Not even if Franny and whichever is there too? Maybe.

Finally we settle on Franny cooking and her asking Phil, because Phil and her aren't in much and they usually go to his place anyway. At last, a solution that feels like a treat for all of us.

The trouble is, Luke is putting up some resistance. I

can't get him to commit himself to the appointed date and every time I bring the subject up it gets met by a wall of silence. I'm extremely concerned by this turn of events, as Luke has yet to meet any of my friends.

The only way is to directly confront him and get to the bottom of the issue.

Are we part of each other's lives or not? I want to know.

Of course we are.

In that case, I would like to move out of this place with just him and me in it and into a wider arena. I want us to be publicly acknowledged. I want him to meet my friends; I want to meet his friends. I don't want this thing between us to exist in this place that has no bearing on the rest of our lives.

Suddenly this feels like the hugest thing, because we are talking level of commitment; because we are tackling the 'how do we feel about each other' stuff; because we are talking about whether this is short-term, mid-term or long-term.

I feel awfully grown up because I never thought about these things before. Before Adam.

Luke and I don't speak for a week.

Then he rings me and says yes, he would love to go to Franny's for dinner.

But I've spent the week telling myself that I have a decision to make in this too, and it's not just about whether Luke is ready for this, it's about whether or not it's right for me to be with someone who has to think about it.

So I tell him the dinner is off and go by myself.

Chapter Six

In which our heroine receives a proposal, gets married, loses a grandfather, attends a dinner party and
endures an uncomfortable lunch with her soon to be
ex-mother-in-law

I have an absolutely marvellous time at Franny's dinner.
I drink lots of wine, talk very loudly, make everyone
laugh a lot, flirt outrageously with Phil, Phil's work
colleague Martin, and Colin the Coke Fiend, Franny's
downstairs neighbour.

But I get hugely disapproving looks from Julie, Martin's 'partner', as she likes to call herself. Then I upset
her even more by declaring loudly, 'Partner? What

does "partner" mean? Whatever happened to a good, old-fashioned boyfriend or girlfriend?'

No one has an answer to this question.

Colin the Coke Fiend saves the day by telling me he saw, 'that bloke I'm seeing' on the telly last week. I give a huge grin of thanks to Colin and a smug smirk to Julie lest she thought my outburst meant that I was a bitter twisted spinster woman doomed to rail for eternity against the fickleness of man. Then I have another glass of wine. Also, I feel bitchily superior to Julie that 'bloke I'm seeing' has a talent that allows him to appear on the telly rather than a talent that locks him up in an office all day making dangerous decisions about other people's money, as does bloke she's seeing.

Franny and Phil are wonderful together. I give Franny lots of affirming hugs at every opportunity and big smiles to Phil, when I'm not flirting.

I'm pleased that I can have a great evening without the promise of sex at the end of it. But the following morning's hangover, with its compulsion to drink gallons of cranberry juice, brings the evening into sharp focus, so I ring Franny to apologise for my embarrassing, over-compensating behaviour, but Franny tells me not to worry, everybody loved me, even Julie.

1992
Whippet trouble

'That bloody bloody dog.'

This is happening too regularly. I go to the Heath, let Harvey off his lead then don't see him for an hour. He is uncontrolled and uncontrollable.

I was told he was untrainable, but only after spending nearly £200 on one-to-one training sessions.

I argue with strangers who berate me for not keeping my dog under control. Some uptight Obsessive Compulsive Disorder sufferer told me to get my dog away from him because it carried diseases, then I told him that he too carried diseases and he threatened to sue me.

I've had to offer to pay dry cleaning bills when Harvey has jumped on picnickers dressed in white after rolling in mud puddles. I've given young children money to buy new footballs. I seem to spend my daily walks on the Heath in a constant state of stress, either apologising to everyone I pass or asking them if they've seen a lost Whippet.

It's not supposed to be like this.

1988
Not how I expected to be proposed to

The M25; now, there was a good idea. Driving back from visiting Maurice one Sunday, Adam and I are slowly edging our way towards North London. It is dark. Before us, the only thing visible through the rain-spotted windscreen is miles and miles of little red dots. Looking to the other side of the motorway, the only thing *visible is miles and miles of white dots. Hell must be something like this.*

I lean back in the passenger seat and close my eyes. Then open them again. We could be here for hours.

'All About Eve,' *I say.*

Adam says nothing.

'Come on. We've got to do something while we're stuck here.'

'Eraserhead.'

'Diner.'

'Revenge of the Killer Tomatoes.'

'Some Like it Hot.'

'Terminator.'

'Um. Ryan's Daughter.'

'Thanks. "R" *again. Rosemary's Baby.'*

'Yanks.'

'Do you think we should get married?'

'I'd have thought your family would have had their fill of weddings lately.'

'I'll take that as a yes then, shall I?'

There is a pause, during which I bin all my romantic fantasies involving, well, mostly Montgomery Clift and Elizabeth Taylor and therefore convince myself that this is probably as good as it gets in real life.

'Your turn,' *I say.* '"S".'

Adam smiles and lights a cigarette.

'Stalag 17,' *he says.*

I hit him.

1989
All we wanted was a registry office
then down the pub . . .

I hope Sadie doesn't regret her decision. She's just agreed to move in with Simon – officially join the family – and suddenly she's thrown into the midst of the chaos, confusion and disorganisation surrounding Adam's and my wedding.

She witnesses tantrums and sulkings and shouting and screaming. When is Mother going to learn some adult behaviour?

There is no point in protesting,

'We just want a small wedding.'

And if Adam says once more, 'I just want a registry office and then down the pub,' I shall call the whole thing off.

What we end up with is two hundred and twenty people at a large central London hotel. But at least we remain firm about a weekday lunch.

Mother and Dad suddenly decide to go all Jewish about it and insist on Kosher caterers and inviting the rabbi. What rabbi? I don't think they can quite believe that I'm marrying someone Jewish. Come to think of it, neither can I.

Helena pounces on the occasion as a public relations opportunity for the business, conveniently forgetting that only nine months previously Julian's wedding had provided a similar arena. These are people that Adam has to deal with so somewhere it's justified, but I'm not wholly convinced.

Simon seems to find the whole thing greatly amusing, but he's madly in love so nothing gets to him.

Helena and Melanie become the quality control panel. Nothing gets past them. Due to a distinct lack of children in our family – I refuse to reach far and wide to rent the usual Bo-Peep and Little Lord Fauntleroy look-alikes – I ask only Franny and Kate to be my bridesmaids. Helena and Melanie are appalled. I'm not sure what picture is conjured up for them; maybe they are still stuck in 'actress means loose living' and fear for the men.

I play along for a while, telling them that we are going for the Moll Flanders look, all heaving cleavages, but Adam insists I put them out of their misery because inevitably their misery is his and ultimately it gets passed back to me.

I am trying so hard to enjoy this, but everyone takes it all so seriously.

Particularly Mother.

You should have seen the state she got into when Adam and I said we didn't want a top table. If we have to endure this day, then at least let us sit with our friends. We won that one. Though Helena and Melanie did not think it was right either.

The day is not much better. Helena refuses to smile throughout and even dares to gasp audibly when Franny and Kate walk behind me down the aisle dressed in red.

Mother has a fixed grin on her face the whole day and even achieves a first for her, which is glaring at me whilst smiling. It's an amazing feat.

Adam and I stand in line at the reception while I am introduced to a couple of hundred people I have never seen before. I have to keep reminding myself where we are and why.

At least I manage to get Adam to dance with me. We didn't want dancing, but Mother insisted.

And then Julian gets up to make an unplanned impromptu speech to announce to the gathered that Melanie is expecting a baby. Simon is so furious at this obscenely manipulative act that he then gets up and announces that he and Sadie are getting married.

Helena and Mother are in competition to see who gets the most congratulations. I have this odd feeling that it should have been Adam and me.

When it's all over, I sit at one of the tables playing with my large bouquet of arum lilies.

('You can't have arum lilies they're too funereal.'

'We're Jewish. We don't have funeral flowers.' But then Jews have a lot of strange customs. Jews don't queue; Jews don't do DIY, not if they can GSETDI – Get Someone Else To Do It, and Jews are always taking things back to shops.)

I watch Adam and Toby smoking a joint, Franny and Kate flirting with the waiters and Simon and Sadie still dancing, even though the band packed up hours ago. They look great together. Same good height, same fit build, same dark colour hair, Sadie's curves fitting neatly into Simon's indents, like two pieces of a jigsaw puzzle.

Simon catches me staring and comes over to sit with me. He takes my hand.

'I'm sorry,' he says. 'I was so angry. I couldn't let him get away with it. Cross with me?'

'No. Just jealous.'

'Jealous! Why?'

'Because no one will stop you having the wedding you want.'

'Registry office—'

'—then down the pub! I didn't really want all this, you know.'

'Then you shouldn't have married Adam.'

'I haven't married Adam, though, have I? I've married Helena, Julian and, God help me, Melanie.'

'Three weeks in the Far East should get you out of that one.'

'Not really. Helena's paying for it all.'

'You don't wish—'

'No. We just didn't want anything to change simply because we got married. But it already has.'

'It'll be fine.' Simon hugs me. 'It's been a big day with an even bigger build-up. You'll be fine, you'll see.'

I look over at Adam. He looks like that same disturbing,

wild-eyed boy I saw on the first day of school. And I get the same feeling. There is something strangely compelling about him and I don't think I like him, but then he looks up at me and winks and I think we'll probably be all right.

1989
Me outside a Buddhist Temple; Adam outside a
Buddhist Temple . . .

I don't think I enjoyed the honeymoon. There was far too much travelling involved.

We got some nice photos, though.

Sadie is chatting away. I am looking at her. How can she be being like this? How long does she think she can keep up the pretence of a happy marriage? I have been trying not to see her because when she talks to me, I just look at her and think, 'You're a liar. You're just lying. Everything that comes out of your mouth that is not about why you threw my brother out of his home, is a lie. Because I don't want to know anything else. I don't want to know how Hannah's reading is coming along, or Rufus's potty training or when you're thinking about going back to work. The only thing I want to know is why. Why is this happening? And why is it happening like this?'

But I promised Simon. That was only two weeks ago.

I go to the bathroom. Now I have to say something, because on the wall next to the bathroom used to hang a small painting that Sadie had painted for Simon for their wedding. It was an abstract piece, so only those of us who knew could tell what it was supposed to be. It was very erotic and very passionate and I loved it.

'Where's the painting?' I ask Sadie on my return.

'It's being cleaned,' she answers.

My God, she's cool. You could almost be convinced that nothing was going on. But now I feel daggers have been drawn. The challenge is on.

'Are you seeing someone else?' I ask her.

'Yes,' she says with utter calmness, not even leaving a moment to think about her reply.

'Who?'

I have provoked a reaction at last.

'That's not your concern,' she snaps.

But I can't bear what this feels like for Simon because I can only too readily call up what it felt like for me.

'Does Simon know?'

'Yes. He's known about it all along.'

'All along! How long is "all along"?'

'That's not your business. This is between Simon and me.'

'And whoever you're fucking.'

'They have no part in this conversation.'

Sadie has a weak point. At last.

'That's all very well if you live in a bubble. But I can't believe you are so egocentric to think that your actions don't affect the people around you.'

Sadie turns on me.

'Do you think I'm not taking responsibility for what has happened? You know nothing about me.'

'You can talk to me, you know.'

For a nano-second it looks like she might. But she doesn't. She won't. She can't. Not about this.

1989
Harry couldn't make it to the wedding

'There's a good one of Franny. Would you like a copy of that one?'

'What's that?'

'Shall I get a copy of that one for you?' I say a little louder.

Harry looks at the picture for a long time.

'She doesn't look good in red. Her mother could wear red. But not Franny.'

I thought Franny looked marvellous. So I tell him. Twice.

Harry will not give up the picture or look at any of the others. He is silent for a long time. I sit patiently, occasionally smiling at whoever trundles past. I know most of them by sight by now and a few of them come and chat and I allow them to believe that I have come to visit them too.

'Ooh, are these your wedding photos?'

Harry looks up.

'Hello, Vi.'

'Sit down,' I say to Vi.

Vi slinks into the chair next to me.

'You've had your hair done,' I say.

She places a withered hand just under her ear and pushes up her thinning, blond, Jean Harlow bob.

'It looks lovely,' I say.

Vi has also made herself up. Her eyebrows have been carefully pencilled in and she has added thick eyeliner to her usual blue eyeshadow. Although the line that separates her lips from the rest of her face has long since disappeared, she has made a brave attempt to reinstate it, but the pink lipstick is all over the place. She used to be a Gaiety Girl and she hasn't changed her make-up since.

'All right, Doris?' she shouts at a similarly made-up old lady sitting across the room from us.

'She used to be a Gaiety Girl,' Vi whispers to me, 'so she says. Mind you, if all the girls who said they were Gaiety Girls, actually were, England would have sunk under the weight of them.'

I love Vi. She's so bitchy. I hope I'm that bitchy when I'm eighty. And I love this place. Full of retired performers, Stewart Granger look-alikes still clutching their albums of reviews and shoving them under the noses of anyone who comes near, old dancers – the Vis and Dorises, grande dames of the theatre who in reality never did much more than endless Agatha Christies in weekly rep and then Harry, partner to some of the greatest comics, 'the best straight man in the business', they called him.

Vi enthuses over the photos. Everyone looks gorgeous. Harry shifts uncomfortably in his seat and groans when I ask Vi to join us for tea.

Uncharacteristically, Vi declines and leaves us.

'You were very rude,' I tell him.

'I can't bear her,' he says. He is still holding onto the picture of Franny.

'You can have that if you like.'

I see that Harry has tears in his eyes.

I guess correctly that he wants to talk about Franny's mother. So I sit and listen.

125

∞

Driving down Highgate Road, I spot Kate and Simon leaving the Heath. Baby Bardolph is in a sling. Simon is wearing the sling.

1986
Margie 2: Hattie O

I really enjoy Margie's second wedding. I am so thrilled that I no longer have to spend an evening with James-the-walking-road-map, I don't care who Margie chooses to take his place.

James was always so old. Well, he wasn't really. He was only twenty-three when they got married. She was eighteen and twenty minutes pregnant, as Dad put it.

She lost that baby. It was three years and two more pregnancies before she gave birth.

I didn't see her much at that time. I was at drama school and I loathed James. I was right to: not only was he an unspeakably boring, pompous git, he had this weird delusion that he was fatally attractive to younger women. Eventually his persistence paid off and he managed to find a younger woman who wanted him. So he left Margie to live in Loudwater ('M1, M25, exit at Junction 19, turn left, away from Rickmansworth, then watch out for the sign on the left that's hidden behind a tree') with a nineteen-year-old beauty therapist and never came near Margie or the twins again.

She's lucky to have found Geoff. He doesn't qualify for Mr Dynamic, but that's obviously never been what Margie's wanted.

I think of her at school, how she could have had any boy she wanted; of how she flirted and teased and made herself into a figure to be envied and feared among the girls. And then I look at the men she has settled for. Who envies her now? Margie has never lost her looks or her style and if I don't envy her her men, I know that I shall always covet her wardrobe.

Posing for her wedding photos she puts her arm through mine.

'Happy?' I ask her.

'I was thinking of Silvio,' she says.

I am shocked. We have never discussed this. Since she sent me that letter, she has not mentioned his name.

'I was in love with him, you know.'

'That wasn't love.' I look over at Geoff, fumbling, unconfident but adoring. 'That is.'

'Thanks,' she says and kisses my cheek.

I am looking at that picture of Margie and me now. It's a lovely picture enhanced by the fact that it is ever so slightly out of focus. They are always the best ones. The unposed. The moments caught unawares.

1993
The uncooperative husband

I learn very early on that Adam is never going to help me with my lines. I asked him once, but he didn't seem to understand that I needed to be told if I wasn't getting the words right.

He, of course, may have done this on purpose to prevent me asking him again. If so, it worked. If I had lines to learn, I would do it during the day when I was on my own. When I wouldn't be told to keep quiet. Or, 'Do you have to do that now?'

Adam was never interested in the acting process.

The only process he was concerned with was the one that led to a near state of oblivion.

1965
When Grandpa died

I go to Simon's room and ask him if he'll play doctors and nurses. He tells me not to be so stupid.

So I put on my nurse's outfit and treat my dolls instead. I have them all lying down in a hospital ward, in beds made up from towels stolen from the bathroom. I take their pulse and temperature, write on their charts and give them some medicine if they need it.

Simon puts his head round my door. 'Grandpa's dead.'

'How do you know?'

'I heard Mum on the phone.'

Simon and I sit on the floor in the middle of my ward and wait for Mother to come and tell us the news.

We wait a long time.

'Are you sure?' I ask Simon.

'Yes, of course. I wouldn't make that up, would I?'

We are silent. I go to one of my dolls and place her sheet over her, like I've seen them do in the films on television.

I collect some more toys and sit them down and explain to them that I'm really sorry but we did everything we could. And I assure them that she did not suffer at the end.

'Did Grandpa suffer?'

'I don't know,' answers Simon impatiently.

'What will happen to him now?'

'We'll have to bury him. There'll be a funeral.'

'What will happen to all his books?'

'I don't know.'

Still Mother doesn't come.

The dolls hold a funeral and I bury the dead one under my bed.

'What will happen to Grandma?'

Simon doesn't answer.

I start to cry.

Eventually we go downstairs to find Mother, because Mother has not come to find us. She looks at me and asks why I am crying.

'I hate you and I'll never forgive you,' I tell her, running from the room.

I lie on my bed, sobbing and sobbing.

It is ages before Mother comes.

1978
Delicate negotiations

'Acting? That's not a career.'

'What is it then?'

'It's an excuse for earning a living.'

'What makes you think you're any good at it?'

'This woman who came in to help out with the school play told me. She said it would be a mistake if I didn't do this professionally. I told you that.'

Mother chips in with, 'But your English teacher told you that you had a gift for writing. You don't want to do that for a career.'

Dad and I agree that writing is not a career. But I continue to insist that acting is.

'Why do you think they have Drama Schools?' I want to know. 'And theatres. Or make films?'

No answer.

'You like going to the theatre. It wouldn't be much good if there weren't any actors, would it? Or is it – it's all right for someone else to entertain you, but not your own daughter?'

'If you insist on doing this, then don't expect me to support you. Do you want to spend your whole life unemployed?'

'I won't,' I say.

'Oh, you're so good, so talented, you'll be whisked off to Hollywood to become the next Barbra Streisand.'

'I don't think it's either one or the other,' I try to explain.

Mother, from who knows where, becomes reasonable.

'Why can't you go to University? There's plenty of Universities that do drama degrees. Then at least you'll have a degree.'

'God help us,' interjects Dad.

'I don't want to go to University. I want to stay in London.'

'London has a very good University.'

'I want to go to Drama School.'

'You're behaving like a spoilt child,' says Dad.

'I'm sure you'll still be able to hold up your heads among your friends. You'll have one graduate child. To ask for two is just being greedy.'

Dad throws his eyes to heaven. He is not, so far, impressed with Simon's University career.

'Well, let's see if any of them will accept you first,' Dad finally concedes. 'If they don't, you'll apply for University.'

I sit back in my chair with a victorious smile on my face, secure in the knowledge that somewhere in London is a Drama School which will take me.

❧

Sadie is becoming more and more distant. There is no semblance of us as a family at all. I have my time with the kids, as does Simon. I can't see how they are ever going to overcome this. Sadie has put up too many barriers. I tell her.

'What you're really saying is I'm putting up barriers to you.'

'If you like.' I'll concede her that one.

'This isn't about you, you know.'

'Why does everyone keep saying that? You are still part of the family whether you like it or not. I don't understand why you are cutting yourself off.'

'You're divorced. You, of all people should know how I feel.'

I am shocked. I've never looked at it like that before. I think about how I feel about the Levys. I shudder.

'Have you never liked us?'

'It's not that. Don't be like that.'

'I've had two sisters-in-law, right? Do you see me spending time with Melanie, ringing her up, going shopping together, or even having any affection for her children?'

'I know. But Hattie, you are doing it again.'

'What?'

'Making it about you.'

'Well, if you refuse to talk about what's going on for you, then one of us has to be in this conversation.'

'You're right.'

'I am?'

Sadie says nothing.

'I really do care—' I start to say.

'Don't tell me you care,' Sadie speaks over me. 'You might think you do. But it's only Simon you really care about.'

'That's not true—'

Sadie speaks over me again.

'And don't say that's not true.'

Why do I feel five years old?

∞

I float around the supermarket in an absolute daze, but bump back to earth when I'm asked to part with £73.08 at the till. What could I possibly have bought?

When my mind is this distracted I really should not do anything that involves spending money. So I settle down and make a list of things not to do when I'm premenstrual:

Dye hair
Cut hair
Have bikini line waxed
Have legs waxed
Have anything to do with wax
Light a candle
Light a fire

Strike a match
Make a decision
Undo a decision
Answer the phone
Answer the door
Answer a question
Read
Write
Think
Sleep with an old boyfriend
Sleep with a new boyfriend
Drive or operate machinery
Anything involving small parts
Anything involving a paintbrush
Anything.

Luke turns up. I offer him a drink, then pour the requested orange juice from the carton. Luke informs me that I failed to shake it. So I tell him, in the last hour the carton has been taken off the shelf, placed in a trolley, been wheeled around the supermarket, taken out of the trolley, placed on the conveyor belt, travelled down the conveyor belt, placed in a carrier bag, been put back in the trolley, wheeled to the car, put in the boot, driven home, taken out of the boot and brought into the house where it was taken out of its carrier and put in the fridge. I think it is probably fairly well shaken.

'Don't tell me you can't find anything to be funny about,' he says.

'I'm not funny. I'm premenstrual,' I tell him. But that only makes him laugh even more.

I decide I must think very seriously about Luke and the role he plays in my life. But not while I'm premenstrual.

1994
Lunch with The Acid Queen

Helena slowly lifts the silver fork carrying a small particle of food and carefully places it in her mouth. Her orange lips close over the prongs which she then removes without leaving a mark on the silver. A tiny ball of light bounces off her highly polished forefinger.

I am mesmerised by her movements. She moves her eyes away from her food and onto my face.

'I always thought that one of the strengths of your marriage was that you had such separate interests, led such separate lives.'

Separate sofas, separate dressing areas and separate bank accounts, yes. But separate sex lives?

'Isn't it strange how history repeats itself? I know he's my son, but I can hardly say I'm surprised. They're none of them to be trusted, you know. Husbands. Sooner or later we're all left on our own. And don't think your next one will be any better, because he won't.'

What does she mean 'next one'? No, I can't think like that. That will turn me into her.

'You look tired, dear.' *Helena makes a brave attempt to lift her wine glass to her mouth. She sips silently, then replaces the unmarked glass.*

'Emotional exhaustion, I think.' *I look at my wine glass, with its lipstick print. It's no use; I would never have been the daughter-in-law she wanted.*

'You can't put everything down to emotional exhaustion,' replies the most exhausted woman in the world.

The waiter comes to clear our plates. Neither of us has eaten very much.

'I'm glad we've had a chance to talk.'

I have no idea what she thinks this lunch has achieved.

'Tell me,' she says removing the gold card from her purse and placing it between the covers of the leather folder containing the bill, 'how do you get on with my husband?'

'Very well.' Her only reaction is an almost imperceptible widening of her irises.

There is absolutely no need to continue the deception. We have both been lied to and betrayed by Adam. Now Helena and I are equal.

I wake up in a disappointment bordering on fury that I am to spend yet one more Sunday morning alone. Luke is somewhere in the Highlands. What on earth use is there in having a lover if he cannot help to indulge Sunday morning fantasies? Everyone knows Sunday mornings are made for sex, yet I have persistently involved myself with men who don't know this. Or, if they do, they are doing it with someone else.

I pick up the papers and find yet another article on the enigma that is Kristen Scott Thomas. If she really wants us to believe that she is an enigma, then she must refrain from agreeing to interviews and from spreading herself over the covers of every available publication.

I pass the mirror on my way to the bathroom and

study the position of my cheekbones. It's no good, I will never look like, or get parts like, KST unless plastic surgery can heighten them. Oh God – I might end up looking like Nancy Reagan instead – this would not be a good thing.

No. I'm stuck with the face I was born with. Anyhow, complete anaesthetic phobia prevents even the contemplation of medical interference. So I have settled instead for improving my skin quality by a rigorous beauty regime involving many different and very expensive creams. Then I was told by Franny last week that cold water is the best thing for skin first thing in the morning. I tried it. She's right. As long as I then use the best moisturiser on the market, I will continue to do this. I make a mental note to visit Harvey Nicks to search for the best moisturiser on the market. Then I remember they are now open on Sundays.

Perfect.

Chapter Seven

In which our heroine has her hair cut, visits her
ex-father-in-law, regrets lost opportunities, finds
something alarming under Kate's bed and falls in
love

Of course, every girl knows the only thing to do in a
crisis is have your hair cut. My hair seems to be getting
shorter and shorter and I'm in danger of being mistaken
for a diesel dyke – so I'm overcompensating by wearing
floaty, flowery dresses and very red lipstick.

I'd completely forgotten that I'm a sometime actress
and when my agent rings (I'd completely forgotten I
had one) to tell me she is finally retiring and she's sorry

but she can't make alternative arrangements for me, i.e. from now on I will not only be jobless and agentless but completely prospectless too, I enter a depression blacker than the latest perfect black top bought in the Joseph sale made from a fabric apparently immune to bleach and therefore supposed to stay black and perfect for ever.

Fortunately it was just a big hype and, as my perfect black top gradually fades to very dark charcoal grey, so does my depression. But my hair is still getting shorter and shorter.

I should really have new photographs taken, as any prospective employer would ball out his personal assistant for inviting a Steve McQueen in *Papillon* look-a-like when a pre-Raphaelite beauty was called for.

I know, I'll ask Simon to take them.

1966
Colour television

'Yes, yes. I can definitely see something.'

'What?'

'Can't you see? There's a definite pink tinge.'

'No, there isn't.'

'Hattie, why do you always have to contradict everything?'

'I don't.'

Simon comes in.

'Quick, quick, you'll miss it,' Dad says to him.

'You're not going to be able to see anything,' Simon tells us.

But Mother insists.

'Can't you see it, Simon? It's definitely not just black and white. There is a hint of colour.'

'I don't see how there could be,' says Simon.

'I'm bored. We've been staring at this stupid thing for hours.'

'Just because they're showing something in colour, doesn't mean we can see it.'

'But I can see it,' says Mother.

Then Simon tells us the awful truth.

'We've watched films that were made in colour on the telly, haven't we?'

Mother opens her mouth to speak. Then changes her mind. Dad sucks on his pipe thoughtfully.

'They weren't in colour when we watched them, were they?'

I watch Mother and Dad for a reaction. Mother is beaten. Dad just listens.

'So, just because they're trying out a colour transmission, why should we be able to see colour?'

I stand up, smiling triumphantly. Mother is proved stupid.

'Can I go now?' I ask.

'I'll make some tea,' says Mother.

1993
'The proper basis for marriage is a mutual misunderstanding'

Everyone said this was the horrible bit, but I'm quite enjoying it. It will be good to have only my things around me. To have a living room that is not dominated by expensive home entertainment equipment. To have shelves that are not displaying records, CDs or videos. Not to have any ashtrays or slowly yellowing walls. To have *a coffee table that does not permanently have on display Adam's drug box. Only my dirty clothes in the dirty linen basket. Never having to iron anyone else's shirts. Being able to cook aubergines, use vege-mince, make spaghetti bolognese with real tomatoes instead of just throwing a bottle of Dolmio over mince (the only way Adam liked it). Never ever to watch another football match. Or listen to an Eric Clapton album. Or suffer a Levy family meal.*

And the really good bit: never having to make myself upset wondering why I wasn't getting the attention I thought I was due. You know, the normal, everyday things like 'hello', 'how are you', 'you look nice', 'I'll help you with that', 'let's—', 'why don't we—?'

It's quite easy to divide things up. Anything culturally sophisticated, literary, artistic, tasteful or to do with Bob Fosse, is mine. Anything subcultural, rock music related or a video of 'One Hundred Best Goals' is Adam's.

He also wants a rather nice, handpainted china tea service. I can't imagine why, but it's fair because I get all the garden pots and furniture and most of the moveable plants that Adam wouldn't even have thought of taking.

But there's the problem of Harvey.

Strictly speaking, he's my dog. I've walked him every day for three years, paid for his food, his vet and grooming bills and kennel fees, kept him worm and flea free, suffered a mud- and dog hair-infested back seat of my car and let him sleep on my pillow every night, severely restricting my breathing.

Nevertheless, he still feels like part of my life with Adam. I wanted a dog, but until you have one you can't possibly be aware of how troublesome they are. And moving into my home that is going to be free from all things to do with my life with Adam, I am reluctant to allow Harvey into it. Much as I love him, and I do, I want my life to change. I want to be able to go out for more than five hours at a time. I want to be out all night – if I want.

I want to feel free.

Adam does not even mention having him. He just assumes that I will take him. I wouldn't want Adam to have him. He can't even look after himself. And as long as he's assuming that Harvey is my responsibility, then I can feel justified in making the decision I'm about to make.

So I telephone the Whippet Rescue Home to register one neutered three-year-old dog looking for a new home. Auf Wiedersehn Pet.

'You were way out of line.'

'It was only a comment.'

'No. I know you. You were trying to be funny. Well, don't use my daughter for your try-outs. Five-year-olds take things very seriously.'

'Sadie, I think you're over-reacting.'

'I am not!' She screams at me. 'Hannah is distraught. In one fell swoop you've shattered all her childhood illusions. What has she to believe in now?'

'Woah! I never said a thing about the tooth fairy. In fact—'

'Shut up, Hattie. Just shut up.'

'No, I won't. You've got this all wrong. Hannah asked me what praying was. And I said it was asking someone who may or may not exist for something you've got no chance of getting. And she said to me, "You mean like Father Christmas?" So she's already doubting his existence.'

Sadie has not been listening. Her hands are covering her eyes. She removes them and looks at me. She's been crying and I suddenly realise this has nothing to do with Hannah at all. Or me.

I move across the sofa to her. She flinches, then relaxes and lets me hug her.

'It's over, isn't it?'

She says nothing.

'He'll come back, you know.'

'Oh, God. I've made such a mess of things.'

'Simon has been waiting for this. It will be fine. You'll work it out.'

It's automatic talk. The things you say at these times. We both know that. And we also both know it may not be quite so easy.

The phone rings.

'Hello?'

'Turn on the television.'

'What?'

'Turn on the television. Channel 5. Quickly.'

'OK. Hold on.'

I leave Franny dangling and hunt for the remote control.

'Right. Got it.' The television bursts into life. 'Oh, my God. I don't believe it.'

Franny is laughing wildly down the phone.

'It's amazing,' she's squealing. 'Did you know anything about this? How did he get this job? He looks ridiculous. This is so weird.'

I can't answer her questions. I am in a state of shock.

It seems that my ex-husband has given up the jewellery business and found a new career as a television presenter on one of those weird late-night 'Generation X'-type programmes.

'I'll phone you back.'

I put down the phone and sit perched on the edge of the sofa. Adam is interviewing some wasted-looking youth about his sudden rise to pop stardom. Adam is looking fairly fit. His face has slimmed down. He is wearing jeans, Levis I assume, he never wore anything else, plain white T-shirt and black leather jacket. His hair has been well cut, about seventy quid's worth at a guess. He is confident and quick and cleverly sits facing the audience so the more famous guest sits in profile towards him. Every so often Adam makes a crack and looks to the camera directly. There is no doubt who is in charge here, whose show this is.

The phone rings.

'Hello?'

'Have you got the telly on?'

It's Kate.

Over the next twenty minutes almost everyone I know phones me. By the third call I've left the answer phone on and gone to bed.

1994
Bognor Regis: where time stands still

'Here, sit down.'

Maurice moves a pile of books away from the worn armchair. I sink, literally, into it. Maurice looks concerned then relieved at my giggle.

'Perhaps over here would be better,' he says, leading me towards the polished mahogany dining table that is never used for its intended purpose. He moves another pile of books and papers.

'Sorry,' he says.

'Don't worry. It's just like my flat. Makes me feel quite at home.'

Maurice smiles.

'I'll get the tea.'

While he's gone I look around the familiar room. Nothing changes here. Except for the view out of the window. Now, in early spring, the plants are tantalising with their promise of summer colour. Every moment brings a new leaf into bud. Here you can watch the seasons change.

On the old sideboard amongst books, papers, plates and decanters is a picture of a young Helena in a tarnished silver frame. I always wonder why he keeps it. It is a beautiful picture. After the war Helena was a model and even had a flirtation with the movies. For a while she was a Rank Starlet. Maurice's photo is a studio portrait. Helena was very beautiful.

Maurice comes back with a tray of tea things.

'She was lovely then, wasn't she?'

Maurice doesn't reply, just places the tray on the table.

When he finally looks at me to hand me a cup of tea he says, 'Oh, you mean she doesn't look like that now?'

I start to laugh. Maurice is obviously upset.

'I'm sorry. I—'

'It's not important.'

But I understand how easy it is here to forget that time moves on. Outside, things change. People get older. Then I see that Maurice

144

has cocooned himself in the same way that Helena has – barricaded himself against other people, the world.

'I'm so sorry about you and Adam, you know.'

'Yes, well. Thanks. But it's better this way.'

'I blame myself, you know.'

'What? Why?'

'If I'd been there—'

But I understand these things now.

'You couldn't live with Helena any more than I could live with Adam.'

'No. I couldn't live with her.'

'And you're not responsible for Helena's reaction. If anyone's to blame, it's her.'

'Adam doesn't like her very much, does he?'

'Adam doesn't like himself very much.'

I look over at the kind, round face.

'I never really knew why—?'

'Why I left?'

'Yes.'

There is a silence in which I watch Maurice weighing up whether to tell me about it or not. He decides not.

'It was all a very long time ago.'

But there are things I need to know.

'Who told Adam?'

'Who told Adam what?'

'How did he know? Who was it who told him that lying and cheating and betraying was OK? Who?' *I have tears in my eyes. This isn't what I meant to say.*

'I'm sorry.' *I compose myself. I look up at Maurice. He has tears in his eyes too.*

'Oh, Hattie. I had no idea. I'm so so sorry. You poor thing.'

Then Maurice and I hug each other and I sob in his arms for hours.

❦

'What's going to happen about Hannah's birthday?'

Simon opens his mouth then closes it.

'You know something dreadful? I honestly don't know.'

'It's a potentially dangerous situation.'

'I don't think there's any need to over-dramatise.'

'Well, Mother and Dad will want to be there, of course.'

'Yes, well that's fine. Hattie, this really isn't your concern. We'll work it out.'

I haven't seen or spoken to Sadie since our last chat.

'Have you had any more sessions – you know?'

'The couple counselling?'

'Yes.'

'No.'

'Oh.'

'Why, "Oh"?'

'Have you spoken to Sadie recently?'

'No. Have you?'

'Me? No. Yes. A few days ago.'

'Yes, well, me too. A few days ago.'

'Did she say anything about . . . anything?'

'About what?'

'I don't know. Anything.'

'No.'

'No. To me neither.'

'You know something.'

'No, I don't.'

'Yes, you do.'

'What? Like what?'

'I don't know. But you do.'

'I don't.'

'OK. If that's how you want to play it.'

'Play what?'

'Come on, Hats. You're not that good an actress.'

'That's not what *The Times* said about my Miss Julie.'

'Fuck Miss Julie.'

Oh-oh. The game's gone too far. I try to make amends by sticking my tongue out slowly. Simon responds, as I hoped he would, doing that Joel Grey in *Cabaret* thing – sticking out his tongue then moving it up to touch his nose.

'Oh, Yeuch!'

'You're only jealous because you can't do it.'

'Yes. Just think of the jobs I've lost by not being able to touch my nose with my tongue.'

'So, what is it you know?'

'It's not up to me to say.'

Simon suddenly looks very concerned.

'Don't worry. Just talk to her.'

'Yeah, I know. It will be fine—'

1989
Men we wish we'd slept with

The way Franny and I differ from Kate is mainly how we think about men. Kate always has very important, serious, long-term relationships. Franny has mainly one-night stands and I am somewhere in between. Kate is always quite content with whoever she is with. But Franny and I are not.

The night before I marry Adam I ask them, 'Does this mean I'll never go to bed with someone who looks like Kris Kristofferson?'

'With or without the beard?'

'With, of course.'

'Not necessarily,' says Franny, predictably.

'Or Matthew Broderick?'

'It's fucking frightening,' agrees Kate.

'Or my doctor?'

'You don't fancy your doctor?'

'I always have crushes on my doctors. He's gorgeous. He's got this grey beard and little round glasses and looks you right in the eye when he speaks.'

Franny and Kate laugh.

'So that's why you're always down the surgery.'

'Of course.'

'Thank God for that,' says Kate. 'I was beginning to think you were turning into your mother.'

'Oh, God. No. But . . . but—'

'What?' they ask together.

'I've never . . . oh, no. No.'

'What?'

'I've never had a black man.'

'Yes, you have.'

'Who? When?'

'You know. What's his name? The carpenter.'

'Oh, him. He wasn't black. He was light brown. Gorgeous though. That lovely long black hair.'

'And bloody dangerous,' Kate reminds me.

'He was more gorgeous than Adam.'

Franny and Kate look at each other.

'I shouldn't be thinking these things, should I?'

'Of course you should.'

'It's perfectly normal.'

I don't believe either of them.

'It was just sex anyway, wasn't it?'

Now it's mine and Franny's turn to look at each other.

'Just sex?' screams Franny. 'Tell me a better way of spending an evening.'

'You know sex,' I say. 'It's that thing you do where you lose an earring.'

'If you're lucky.' Franny and I get hysterical. Kate gets all tight-lipped.

'Come on, Kate,' I say. 'We're only jealous of your loving, nurturing, giving relationships.'

'Jealous! You're the one that's getting married tomorrow.'

I had forgotten. For a while there I thought I was a single girl. Then I think, oh, well, it won't be for long.

⋙⋘

'Luke has arranged for me to meet his agent.'

'That's so nice.'

'Do you think so? It's a bit controlling, isn't it?'

Kate never sees things like that.

'But his agent is all light entertainment stuff. He doesn't do the other bits. Tellys, films, theatre.'

Kate removes Baby Bardolph from her right breast and places him over her shoulder.

'When was the last time you even went up for a telly?'

'But that's exactly the point. Now Senile Susie is finally giving up, I should be finding an agent that will send me up for those things. But Luke is so fixated on me doing this comedy thing.'

Baby Bardolph expels enough air to launch the space shuttle.

'Clever boy. Oh, you're such a good, clever, beautiful boy. And I love you.'

'I used to talk to Harvey like that.'

Baby Bardolph is placed on the left breast.

'Hasn't he had enough?'

'My baby never has enough, does he?'

'What do you think?'

'I think you should just go meet this woman—'

'It's a guy.'

'Whoever. And just see what he has to say.'

'Yeah. Hmmm.'

I lie back on the bed whilst Kate continues feeding. I love Kate's bedroom. It's so plain and practical yet calming. Kate's so neat. Even with all the baby's things, there's never anything lying around where it shouldn't be. The floorboards are light and clean, the bed linen crisp and cream. I put my hand out over the end of the bed and run my fingers along the floor as if I am lying in a punt on the river. My fingers touch something. I grab it, assuming it is one of Baby Bardolph's schmutters. (Kate insists on calling them Harrington Squares – she can be so Harrods sometimes.) But what I bring to the surface is a pair of boxer shorts.

I sit holding them, just looking at them, trying to work out a rational explanation. Kate has her eyes closed and gently rocks BB. She hasn't noticed. Should I just put them back and say nothing? Too late. Kate has opened her eyes.

'Ah,' she says.

'Oh,' I say.

'Yes,' she says.

'Right,' I say.

1976
Things that are legal at eighteen

Dad and Simon are arguing. This situation is completely unprecedented so I sit on the stairs listening to the to-ing and fro-ing of their reasoning, knowing that there is no way, at this crucial time, that Dad is going to give in.

'Your Mother and I—'

'Oh, come on Dad. Don't start using Mother in this. This is about what you want to do.'

'Look. You may be leaving home—'

'Oh. At last you're acknowledging that that's what I'm doing. Yes. I'm leaving home. Not living here anymore. Living somewhere else. Going to University.'

'And who is supplementing your grant?'

'Don't pull that one on me. You can't get your own way just because you're paying for me. That's what parents do for their children, support them, provide for them until they can do it for themselves. So don't make me feel guilty about that one.'

I admire Simon's staying power. I would have walked out, slamming doors, long ago.

'You're still only eighteen—'

'Eighteen. I have the vote. I can drink in a pub. I can get

married without your permission. The only thing I cannot do is legally indulge in homosexual sex.'

There is a silence. Simon has to give in now by way of apologising for going too far.

I am wrong. It is Dad who speaks first.

'All I'm doing is offering to help you move your things. I'm sorry if you consider that intrusive on your new life. You do it your way.'

'No, Dad. I'd really like you and Mother to take me down to Sussex. But Hattie doesn't have to come too, does she?'

1986
. . . I'll do it tomorrow

This is fine, isn't it? OK, we're both tired. It's been an exhausting day. It's been an exhausting few weeks.

All that dealing with estate agents and building societies and surveyors and builders, damp proof experts and removal firms. Not to mention packing up all my stuff in endless boxes. Adam doesn't seem to have half as much stuff as I do.

And then the organising the boxes into rooms and the bits of furniture that we've been given; a sideboard, a library table and two bookshelves from Dad and four non-matching dining chairs, a footstool and a fender from Maurice. All the other furniture is mine because Adam was living in rented accommodation so he didn't need any. The bed, the sofa bed, the chest of drawers and the Edwardian pine wardrobe – the essentials – all supplied by me.

Not to mention the crockery, cutlery, pots and pans. I seem to have collected a lot in the ten years since I left home.

The kitchen is almost up and working. Everything has been

unpacked. The bed has been assembled and made. Most of the clothes are hanging in the wardrobe. Adam says that, as I've taken up most of the fitted wardrobe in our bedroom, he will take over the second bedroom for his clothes.

But I thought we were going to use that as the dining room.

What do we need a dining room for? Adam wants to know.

The answer is simple. To eat in.

So the Edwardian Pine Wardrobe and chest of drawers has been put in the second bedroom.

The living room looks unbelievable. Boxes and furniture have just been abandoned. We can't face doing anything more tonight. Well, we've got the whole weekend. Best get to bed.

First night in new flat together. Our new home. Ours. A home that Adam and I have bought together because we want to be together. Live together. Some sort of affirmation of all that is surely on the cards.

But no.

Adam has gone to sleep.

I refuse to consider this any kind of omen or listen to the wail of the alarm as it rings right in my ear.

Your first night in your first home and you don't have sex.

That's because, I convince myself, we don't need to. This is so right, so comfortable, so easy, there's no need for confirming gestures. We know.

Don't we?

I've fallen in love with Aidan, Luke's agent. This could be a disastrous situation if his agent were available, straight and interested. It's easy to find out the answer to the first two. So I simply ask Luke, who wonders why I want to know, do I fancy him or something? I can't possibly tell him the truth, so I just pretend that these are the sort of details I like to know about someone if they are to become my agent. Characteristically male-like, Luke doesn't know the answers to these basic questions as his agent's private life has never concerned him and he doesn't understand why it should concern me.

So no joy there.

I invent a reason for dropping in on Aidan with a video tape of a performance I had not wanted him to see, but the opportunity to give it to him, therefore allowing me a second chance to check him out, is worth the embarrassment of the substandard performance he may have to endure. Was he really as devastatingly attractive as I first thought?

Shit! He is!

He is also charming and hospitable considering the unplanned intrusion on his time. In fact, he is so pleased to see me he invites me out for a coffee, then and there. Naturally I decline and tell him I have to dash for an appointment. He seems genuinely distressed. He promises to view the tapes as soon as possible and extremely daringly, considering he knows the situation between Luke and me, invites me out for a drink.

I still don't know whether he is available or straight, but Aidan certainly seems interested.

I leave his Berwick Street office and head straight for the tube without even considering a quick look round the shops. But I only realise this when I get home. I regret the missed opportunity to spend money, but feel awfully glad that I didn't feel the need for a displacement activity. So I settle down with a book but don't take in any of it – I elaborate a fantasy about Aidan instead.

I'm so involved in my Aidan fantasy that I completely forget I am supposed to meet Simon after work to talk about my new photos.

I've never ever done that before.

Shit! Might be serious, this one.

Chapter Eight

In which our heroine believes she has found the
perfect new man, but has to get rid of the old one first,
fails to buy a new dress for her brother's wedding,
gets a love bite and dresses to kill

I'm feeling like shit, the planets must be in complete
turmoil to be causing so much havoc in my life. Over
the past week I've upset Simon by forgetting to meet
him, distanced Luke by my own distancing behaviour,
forgot to send a birthday card to Margie, then had
to grovel for forgiveness which was not forthcoming,
received an unfair tax bill, got told off by Dad for not
asking after Mother's health (I can't even remember

what new affliction she's suffering from), dropped and broke the new Conran Shop perfect salad bowl which was supposed to be Margie's birthday present and, to put the lid on it, I saw Toby and Grace together in a trendy Crouch End café – I haven't spoken to or heard from either of them in nearly a year. I was not going to speak to them, but the size and shape of Grace's extended stomach, something I couldn't possibly ignore, meant I had to say something.

I came away feeling unclean, so I stopped at a florist on the way home and bought twenty pounds'-worth of large wild flowers to fill the empty vase in the living room, cover up a large expanse of empty wall space and feed my empty soul.

I brood all day over the meeting with Grace and Toby and the awkwardness it produced and even though I have my own life now, that I am partially contented with, I still feel excluded from my other life that, had things been different (they would have to have been very different), I should ideally still be living.

1993
Who'd like to be mother?

Jan comes over to me as I wash some glasses. She picks up a tea towel and starts to dry them. Jan is very good at not taking much space, despite her weight, and I am always grateful for this.

'There's no need.'

'It's all right.'

'OK then.'

We are silent until the fourth glass.

'Don't say anything to anyone and don't let Grace know I told you, but we're thinking of having a baby.'

I get cross at her assumption that it is going to be easy, but it is for most people – it just wasn't for me and Adam. But Jan and Grace having a baby summons up farcical images of turkey basters – they are already at a disadvantage.

'How?' is the stupid question I ask. 'I mean, have you thought about who is going to father it, or are you going to go to a Donor Clinic?'

'We're still discussing it.'

'And which one of you will have it?'

'Grace wants to.'

I am surprised by this. Not that Jan and Grace play out male/female roles, but Jan is infinitely more feminine, soft, motherly. Grace is hard, or so she would have us all believe.

'I think it's marvellous news.'

I turn to Jan and give her a hug.

'I know this might be hard for you, so I wanted to tell you first.'

'Thanks. But it's fine. I'm passed all that.'

I look out into the garden at Adam and Grace, who are studying his drugs box, the contents of which never cease to amaze Grace. I know it's over. I know it's only a matter of time before we make it happen.

'It was just as well – any offspring of Adam's would be letting the human race down. It would be a step backwards, evolutionally speaking.'

Grace looks up and sees me watching. She doesn't smile, just turns back to Adam. I wish she didn't make me feel so uncomfortable.

The door bell rings.

'That'll be Toby,' I say and go to let him in.

'Another?'

'Yes. Please.'

'The same?'

'Yes. Thanks.'

'I'll make it a double, shall I? Then it will last longer.'

'Or get me pissed quicker.'

Aidan takes my empty glass and goes to the bar, giving me the perfect opportunity to study his physique. Nice broad shoulders. Slim waist and hips, but not too slim, and buttocks not too tight. Fit but not muscular. Well groomed, nicely dressed, great haircut, nice shoes and plain socks. Men should only wear patterned socks if they come from Paul Smith. Also, he's tall without being overpowering. And I love the dark hair, green eyes combination. No wedding ring. No jewellery at all. Good. There's no doubt about it – he's practically perfect.

There's got to be a catch.

'Here you are.'

'Thanks.'

He sits back down opposite me.

'You'll have to have some new photos done.'

'Yes, I know. My brother's supposed to be doing them. But ... oh, it doesn't matter. It's boring and complicated.'

'What is?'

'Nothing.'

'Tell me. I'm interested.'

My God. I really think he is!

I give him a brief synopsis of the Simon/Sadie/Kate/ Hannah/Mother/Dad scenario. All the way through, he doesn't take his eyes off me. The story starts to garble by the end, then wind down until finally I come to a complete standstill and Aidan is still looking at me. I'm not one for blushing, but I know my cheeks are burning. There is a silence. We are staring into each other's eyes.

'You fascinate me.'

'So, are you married or gay or what?'

Aidan roars with laughter.

'You're marvellous,' he says and takes my hand, turn- ing my insides into a liquid that floods my knickers.

'Neither,' he says, then places his mouth on my already open one.

1990
If you could see her through my eyes

All day I feel guilty. But Simon and Sadie don't know the difference. I feel that because I didn't buy a new outfit that means I'm making some kind of comment. They don't know. They've never seen this dress before. They don't know that I've borrowed the hat from Franny, that the shoes, although hardly worn, were not specially bought to go with the dress. Maybe I am making some kind of comment. Of course I am. I'm saying 'I don't think enough of the occasion of your wedding to go out and buy something especially for it.'

Mind you, neither does Simon.

Mother buys a new dress but wears an old hat and Dad never buys anything new.

None of us make much of an effort really. None of Sadie's immediate family are there. Australia is a long way to come just for a wedding. But her mother's sister, Sadie's Aunt Bella, stops off in London from her round the world trip to attend the big, or rather small, day.

Dad loathes Bella on sight. She is everything he hates: loud, vulgar, rude and overbearing.

Simon is in shock at the sight of her and Sadie simply embarrassed. Bella insists on being in every single photograph so she has a plentiful supply to show the family back home.

Simon and Sadie want a quiet family lunch. They are having a party for their friends in the evening. So Simon, Sadie, Adam, me, Mother, Dad and Bella go for lunch at the Belvedere in Holland Park.

Bella does nothing to revise Dad's opinions of Australians. Even worse, she reinforces every worst stereotype. It is most unfortunate. But who should turn out to be the hero of the day?

Adam turns on the charm, plays his man-of-the-people act and succeeds in reducing Bella's audience to just one – him. It is miraculous, the way he handles it. By the end of the lunch the two of them are inseparable, conversing in conspiratorial whispers and leaving the rest of us to chit-chat about nothing, just like any other family gathering. Mother keeps stealing glances at the odd couple. I believe she is a little put out. Adam's attention is generally on her. And now she has a rival.

This is so ridiculous. Now Mother has actually started to sulk.

Simon looks over to me and I give him a 'I-can't-believe-she's-behaving-like-this' look back.

Dad is going on about something or other. Prattling on as usual, not directing his speech at anybody in particular, but always just assuming that someone at some point is going to be listening and will respond. It's usually me, saying something like, 'What nonsense.'

But it's Sadie who pays him the most attention because she's new and she hasn't yet quite sussed out how it all works.

Just your average family gathering.

1990
Prima donnas

Sadie is not fooled by Toby. I have never yet witnessed anyone so blatantly disapprove of him.

As I wander past them, I can hear Toby repeating the tale he told me ten minutes previously.

'So I told them if they wanted me to be in peak condition for the opening night, then they must put up with me not giving my all at rehearsals. It's an exhausting, demanding role. Either they want me to be good, or they don't. I can't risk my voice.'

'Opera singers never go to rehearsals at all,' Sadie is telling him. I see a look of panic cross Toby's face. I don't think he wants his perfectly reasonable behaviour associated with the prima donnas of the opera world. So he ignores her and carries on: 'And then the wardrobe girl comes in with this thing and I said, "You can't expect me to wear that."'

'Does she have a name?' asks Sadie. I love her.

Toby ignores her again.

'And she said that we open in three days and I couldn't expect her to find me a whole new costume in that time, what with everything

else she had to do. And I told her that it was her job to do just that. Can you believe her attitude?'

Toby waits for approval from Sadie, then he catches me listening in to their conversation. Sadie uses me as an excuse to go and attend her other guests. Toby seems unfazed but, as his audience has gone, he continues to tell me the story he has already told me, ten minutes before.

'You know that scene in *Annie Hall* when they're making love and she gets up, leaving her body there for him?'

'Yes?'

'You just did that.'

I turn over to Luke and nestle against his chest. His arms are folded behind his head so I have a clean run of licking him from nipple to arm pit. He doesn't respond.

'I'm sorry.'

'I'd honestly rather you just said you didn't want to, than have it like that.'

'I'm sorry.' I nip at his shoulder.

'Cut it out.'

'I'm sorry.'

'So what's on your mind?'

'Just a bit distracted.'

'Do you want to talk about it?'

What I wouldn't have given to have had Adam ask me that. But, grateful as I am, I decline.

'Whatever,' says Luke. He gets up.

'Where are you going?'

'To get a drink.'

'Oh. I thought you might—'

He comes back and sits on the bed.

'I am not any of those bastards, you know.'

No – but he has his moments though.

'I love the nineties. Relationships are so different than they used to be. I mean, if you can have a successful non-committing relationship, well you've got it made. Cake, cake, cake – whenever you want it.'

'I thought there was something.'

He slides back into bed.

'Sometimes I need some reassurance.'

'Premenstrual?'

'Fuck off.'

Luke goes to get a drink.

There wasn't really anyone else other than Adam all through school. I maybe snogged a couple of boys at a party, maybe went on one or two 'dates'; to the cinema or something. Adam and I didn't go out that often, perhaps ice skating or boating on the pond at Regent's Park.

I just didn't do that boy thing; not in the way Margie did, anyway.

My feelings for Adam blew hot and cold. If he was pestering me to go out with him, I would decide I didn't fancy him and turn him down. If he ignored me, I would decide I was madly in love with him, doodle his name all over my exercise books and even once scratched his initials on my arm.

Often we would be at the same club or concert, but we'd be with other people and not speak to each other. And of course I saw him every day at school.

That was a lot of days seeing him every day.

I don't miss him.

1976
That must have been one hell of a mosquito

The water feels cold as I wriggle my toes in it. A diagonal line cuts the pool in half as the sun moves behind the apartment block. I am sitting in the shade, reading as I wet my feet. Round my neck I have a scarf and I'm wearing a T-shirt over my swimsuit. The scarf is attempting to cover up a love bite. It's a pathetic attempt. Everyone knows. Everyone can see it. Amazingly, Mother has said nothing.

Her and Dad have pretty much left me alone this holiday.

Which is why I have this thing on my neck. I got it from Jean-Pierre. He wanted me to have sex with him, but I said no. We were snogging last night in the room behind the pool where they store the mattresses.

'Lie back,' he said.

'No,' I said.

He wants a pair of my knickers. He says he collects them. I think this is horrible. But I give him a pair – a really nasty pair – a pair that are old and falling apart and very unsexy. I don't think that's quite what he had in mind.

The next day I see him explaining the workings of his camera to a young pretty French girl. He doesn't even look up as I walk past. Either time.

But I still have this thing on my neck.

❧

I sit up and push Aidan away.

'Oh, no! This is terrible.'

Aidan takes my hand and pulls me back towards him.

'Look, we have to stop.'

Aidan's lips seem permanently stuck to my neck.

'I mean it,' I shout.

Aidan removes himself and sits back, waiting for me to say something. Or do something.

'Talk about the casting couch.'

'Is that what you think this is?'

'I don't know. I don't know anything about you. Except—'

'What?'

I look into those emerald eyes.

'This feels so weird.'

'Good weird or bad weird?'

'Lovely weird.' I feel myself falling towards Aidan. He puts his arms out to catch me. I love that. I lean against him. He lifts both hands and places them around my head, holding my head in his hands. He bends his head and kisses my eyes, my nose, outlines my lips with his tongue. His hands have moved to hold my neck. He shifts his position. He now looms over me and I get an overwhelming sense of protection. His arms encircle my

167

body and he holds me tightly against him, still kissing my face, then very very gently places his lips directly on mine. Now I can respond, hoping that my kiss feels as good to him as his does to me. Considering that he doesn't pull away, I shall assume it does.

But I am still not ready for more. This is most unlike me. What on earth can be going on?

But I know. It's Luke.

I pull away.

'I have to sort things out with Luke.'

'Good. I'd rather you would, if you want me to be honest with you.'

IF I WANT HIM TO BE HONEST WITH ME!?

'I hope you will be.'

'And you with me.'

'I hope you're prepared to give up some cells for cloning because I know several women who'll want someone just like you.'

Aidan smiles.

'Let's go eat.'

1979
Ip dip Sky Blue

Naturally, Franny doesn't see a problem. I knew I shouldn't have told her about it. It's not as if it's a problem as such. If I'm being honest, I like the idea of there being two men who want to sleep with me. I think it would be really cool if I managed to sleep with them both in the same week, or on consecutive nights, or even on the same day. I think I would love that.

I know Tom is sleeping with Lorri sometimes, so if he can sleep with two people, I can. And nothing has happened yet with Rueben. He's only offered to take me for a ride on his motorbike. Of course, if it came to it I would sleep with him. I mean, he's so cute. He's got this dead sexy Spanish accent and he's not full of shit like most of the other guys on the course. Of course, him not being English means he doesn't get the parts he should – the parts equal to his talent.

I wouldn't even have thought about him like that if he hadn't asked me to come for a ride with him then suddenly I thought, oh my God, he's gorgeous. I could do this if I wanted. And I might.

Franny says, what on earth am I dithering about, just fuck the guy, she would. (Later I find out she did.) But I'm not as experienced or as confident as she is. Yet.

I think I may simply enjoy the idea of being able to do it if I wanted, but something tells me I won't quite have the guts to see it through. And Tom is showing signs of possessiveness. This is more flattering than alarming.

For God's sake – a ride on the back of a motorbike isn't going to do any harm.

'You have two messages. Hear them?'
   'Yes.'
   'Sorry. I didn't understand that. Hear them?'
   'Yes, you deaf bitch.'
   'Sorry. I didn't understand that. Hear them?'
   'Yes.' I scream down the phone.
   'Message received at 18.46. Play?'

'Yes. Jesus, this woman gets on my nerves,' I tell Luke. 'She must be raking it in, though. Why couldn't I have got a job like that?'

'It isn't a person. It's a computer.'

'Really? Ssh.'

'Hi, Hattie. Can you have Hannah on Friday afternoon? If you could have her to stay over that would be marvellous. Rufus is going to your Mum's. Look, come over for lunch on Friday, if that's OK. We'll talk then. Bye.'

'Repeat?'

'No.'

'Remove?'

'Yes.'

'Message saved.'

'I said yes, "remove" you stupid . . . She's not a very efficient computer. I could have done a much better job.'

'Message received at 2020. Play?'

'Yes.'

'Aidan here—'

I instinctively turn my back on Luke. I perch on the arm of the sofa. I daren't face Luke. My face is burning hot.

'I'll try again later. Look forward to speaking to you then. Bye.'

The 'Bye' was almost a whisper.

I put the phone down, forgetting that I didn't conclude my interrogation.

'Who was that?' asks Luke as he flicks through *Time Out*.

'Umm. Sadie. Just Sadie. That's all. No one else.'

I slide off the arm onto the sofa next to Luke.

'Aidan's trying to set up a European tour for me.'

'Really. That's great.'

'Why are you laughing?'

'I'm not. I'm happy for you. It'll be fun.'

'He wants me to do all the summer festivals. It'll be about three months on the road.'

'Wow!' I cannot make the grin on my face go away.

'So I'll be gone all summer.'

'Hmmm.'

'Maybe we should—'

'It's all right Luke. I know what you're going to say. And it's fine, really.'

'Oh. Well. Good.'

There doesn't seem much more to say.

'You didn't have to look so pleased about me going away.'

'I'm sorry. I was thinking about something else.'

'You've been doing a lot of that.'

'Yeah.'

'Look. Anything I can help you with, you know, the comedy stuff. I'd still like to see that through with you.'

'Sure.' Why am I not feeling anything?

'I'll go then.'

'There's no need. Stay.'

'P'raps not.'

'Maybe you're right.'

We are standing by the front door now. Before he opens it, I fling myself into his arms. He holds me. We kiss.

'It never really happened between us, did it?'

Can he really mean that?

'I'll always have a lot to be grateful to you for.'

'You'd have got there. You don't need me.'

Why is he being like this?

'I'll call you,' he says, and goes.

As the door closes I feel alternate waves of sadness and relief. And terribly grown up. The phone rings. I run into the lounge to get to it before Computer Bitch.

'Hi.'

'Hi.'

'Good time, bad time?'

'No, it's a good time,' I tell Aidan. 'A very good time.'

1990
'So I'm one of the top five gods . . .'

'I know. I'm Tinkerbell.'

'Yes.'

I remove the Rizla stuck to my forehead. It does indeed say 'Tinkerbell' in Toby's spidery handwriting. Now there's only Adam and Toby left. Adam has 'Spotty Dog' stuck to his forehead and Toby has 'Buddha' stuck to his.

'Right,' says Adam. 'I'm an animal in a children's programme, animated. Am I a cartoon character?'

'No,' we all chorus.

Adam looks non-plussed.

'I just don't know,' says Toby. 'I can't even establish if I exist or not. I know. God. I must be God.'

'No, not exactly.'

'What does "not exactly" mean? Either I'm God or I'm not.'

Jan 'Virginia Woolf' leans over Grace 'Princess Leia's' head, who sits on the floor between Jan's legs leaning against her chair. 'There's more than one god, you know,' she says.

Toby looks shocked. He has evidently never considered this.

'So I am a god?'

'Too late,' I tell him. 'You got a "no". It's Adam's turn.'

Toby leans back in the chair and starts to nervously bite the skin around his thumbnail.

'If I'm not a cartoon, then I must be a puppet.'

'Yes.'

There is a silence. Adam is thinking. As his brain works slower than most people's, this may take some time.

'Hector. Off "Hector's House".'

We all laugh.

'Nice guess,' says Toby. 'But no.'

'Oh.' It obviously took all of Adam's brain power to come up with that one.

'Is that new?' Grace asks, grabbing hold of my wrist as I reach for a crisp.

I hold my arm up then let my hand drop, allowing my white gold bangle with its single inlaid diamond to fall.

'Yes,' I say, already feeling guilty. Grace always makes me feel guilty for having new things. 'Adam got it really cheap because the woman it was made for decided she didn't want it.'

'That's not what happened. She left her husband before he paid for it, so he said he wasn't going to.'

'Stupid woman,' I say. Then I hate myself for sounding so materialistic.

'It's really lovely,' says Grace.

'Thanks.'

'So, if I'm not God, what about Allah?'

'No.'

'Shit.'

'Parsley, the lion.'

'No.'

'I can't think of any more gods.'

'I know – Dylan?'

'No, and it's not your turn.'

'I give up,' says Toby removing 'Buddha' from his head.

But Adam will not.

1980
Thanks so much for coming

'We really enjoyed it.'

'Did you? Really?'

'Yes,' says Margie, her voice wavering slightly.

'I'm so glad you came.'

I really mean this. I've tried to include Margie in my new life at drama school. It's been hard. She's had her own problems, her own life. There have been long gaps when I felt I'd neglected her. We speak on the phone, but we don't see each other very much so I really am glad she came.

James has not said a word. He just stands slightly behind Margie, looking around him and not even attempting to join in our conversation.

'I don't know how you remember all those lines,' says Margie. I laugh.

'I liked, what's her name, the pretty one with the blond hair?'

'Kate. Yes, she's really talented.'

'Oh, that's Kate. The one that's going out with Simon?'

'Yes.'

'Has Simon seen this yet?'

'No. Simon's not very good at coming to see things. He's only been a couple of times.'

'Oh.' Margie is genuinely surprised.

'Well, he lives with us and everything and I suppose he likes to keep a bit of his own life. He doesn't want to be hanging around here all the time.'

'How is he?'

'Simon? All right. Look, do you want to come upstairs for a drink?'

Margie says, 'Yes, that would be lovely,' and James says, 'No we can't, we have to get back,' both at the same time.

Margie looks embarrassed.

'We'd better go,' she says.

'Thanks for coming.' I hug her.

They go. James doesn't even say 'goodbye'.

1979
Knock knock knocking on Hattie's wall

I am having difficulty sleeping.

This has been going on for a couple of months. OK. It's been going on ever since Kate started spending her nights in Simon's bedroom. The bedroom next door to mine. It's not as if I can hear them having sex or anything. That's what's bothering me – that I can't hear them; because if I could I would know that they were and then it would be over and we could all go to sleep. But, because

175

I can't, I'm constantly wondering whether they are, whether it's good, how long it lasts, who comes first . . .

Only Franny knows about my obsession with their sex life and naturally thinks it's very funny. Not odd at all.

'But he's my brother—' I keep telling her, 'and she's one of my best friends. It's so perverse of me. I don't worry about the details of your sex life.'

'That's because you know them all,' replies Franny.

'That's it,' I say. 'It's because they're being so secretive.'

'Perhaps more discreet than secretive. Maybe they're trying to protect your feelings.'

'Why would they do that? What do you mean "protect my feelings"? I don't have a problem about it.'

'No, of course you don't. That's why you're not getting any sleep. That's why you've got bags under your eyes.'

'I don't get it. Simon sees me and Tom together. He knows Tom stays over at our place. I don't get all funny about it. I don't see the need to protect Simon from it.'

'I rest my case,' says Franny.

'What case? What are you talking about?' I am obviously getting hysterical. 'Sorry, I'm getting hysterical. I'll go back to the flat and try to sleep before tonight.'

'But we've got a singing rehearsal in half an hour.'

'Fuck!'

The strange empty feeling I've been carrying around since Luke's departure will not go away, despite an expensive visit to the Garden Centre. My garden now boasts a fragrantly beautiful lavender hedge of alternate blue and white, behind which I have dug over the old vegetable patch and sown and planted a mixture of cottage and wild flowers. I would love a dense bed of hollyhocks, lupins, delphiniums and foxgloves, interspersed with poppies, cornflowers and meadow grass. Now I just have to sit back and watch it grow.

I realise the reason I love gardening is, it's fairly easy. Contrary to popular belief it's actually quite hard to kill a plant, unless the slugs get there first. But now I know what slugs like to eat, I simply don't provide them with ready-made meals. It worked; the slugs have all migrated to neighbouring gardens to feast on hostas and marigolds, whilst my plants remain relatively hole-free. Unlike my life.

Luke has left a bigger hole than I could have predicted. He has rung once or twice, but I feel torn between attempting to continue some kind of vague friendship and the feeling that I never want to see him again. But I must be adult about this. We were both at the same place at the same time and not many people can say that about their relationships – even if it did mean we both wanted it to end.

Aidan, meanwhile, is being enormously attentive. I cannot believe that we have not yet been to bed together. It's only been three weeks, but this is so unlike my usual behaviour that I'm getting seriously concerned about the level of seriousness or, in my more insecure moments, worrying about those things that may prevent him from having sex with me – everything from a potentially fatal sexually transmitted disease to impotence. Or should that be the other way around?

Ah well – I'm seeing him tonight. Maybe I'll wear

the short tight red leather skirt and black lace top.
That should do the trick. I feel absolutely ready for this
now ...

∞

PS It worked ...

Chapter Nine

In which our heroine cannot rid herself of feelings of dissatisfaction, bumps into an old boyfriend at an Art Gallery, enjoys a Greek holiday and tells her father the truth

I hate myself for behaving like a horrid spoilt brat. I've nothing to complain about, but I'm still managing to feel faintly dissatisfied. I've got a gorgeous, practically perfect man behaving in a curiously attentive and devoted manner who not only showers me with compliments, little gifts and great nights out, but is gloriously loving, kind and drop dead sexy(ish) in bed. All too bloody perfect. Not one single alarm bell has rung in all the time (one month) that

I've known him. There is a potential danger area in the shape of his ex-wife, but I have to remind myself that I too am an ex-wife and I have no intention of causing problems in any relationship Adam may choose to involve himself in. But ex-wives can be a chilling reminder of a past in a manner ex-girlfriends can only aspire to.

Funny thing is, I get inexplicably tongue tied whenever I'm questioned on my new man by Kate or Franny or Simon. I simply can't talk about it.

So I ring Margie and ask her to make an appointment for me to have a session with her psychic; I feel the sudden need to know. Before, I've always not wanted to know, assuming it would all end up rotten anyway. But not this time. I need someone else to tell me whether Aidan is worth taking a risk over – I simply can't make that decision by myself.

The wonderful thing about Aidan is that he doesn't give me any opportunity to doubt him; before I've even had time to change the sheets, he's on the phone wanting to see me. It's producing a new sensation which must be something like security. Oh, well. I'll wear it for a while and see how it feels. Knowing how quickly I wear out my knickers, my lipsticks and my shoes, I can't really see this security thing lasting too long.

1992
Never use a two-word title

'Fatal Attraction *started it*.'

'What?'

'You know, the two-word title thing that marked the decline in the standard of the so-called "adult" Hollywood thriller. Two words. Two stars. Huge salaries. Well, I've got two words for them – crap films.'

Toby gets up and passes me as I enter from the kitchen with a bowl of mixed summer fruits.

'Simon's at it again,' he tells me, touching me lightly on the shoulder in a sympathetic sort of way.

'Basic Instinct, Indecent Proposal—'

'Random Harvest, Hello Dolly' shouts Toby from the kitchen.

'Watership Down,' says Grace. 'God, I hate those fucking bunnies.'

'Are you all deliberately misunderstanding me?'

'Simon,' I say softly, handing him a bowl.

'What?' He looks truly frightened for a split second.

'Would you like cream or fromage frais?'

He doesn't understand. He puts the bowl on the coffee table.

'I should go. I'm not good company tonight.'

'Don't be silly,' I say. 'We're thrilled to see you. It's been too long since you saw us all like this.'

'Since Hannah was born,' he reminds us, as if we didn't know.

'Stay,' says Adam. 'It could be years before you're allowed out again.'

I try to catch Adam's eye to make him aware of his tactlessness. But he's oblivious. He thinks he's being funny.

Simon doesn't move. I smile at him.

'Jagged Edge,' I say.

Simon kisses my cheek.

'Jagged Edge was made before Fatal Attraction,' he whispers in my ear. 'But thanks.'

1967
Gather ye heirlooms while ye may

It goes like this: Mother is responsible for my birthday and everyone's Christmas presents, but Dad, and only Dad, gets Simon his birthday present. He never discusses it with anyone, least of all Simon. He has been known to leave the office at lunchtime and wander around the West End's antique shops for hours in search of the perfect present, or his own lost youth, one or the other.

While I have had to settle for a dalek outfit, a pair of stilts, a pogo stick or, on one memorable birthday, a space hopper that lasted approximately three minutes before Dexter attacked it and tore it to shreds, Simon has been gathering heirlooms.

He has three or four exquisite Victorian wind-up toys: a monkey banging cymbals, a soldier beating a drum; he has a rocking horse, with a real horse hair mane; he has a valuable collection of first edition Boy's Own annuals, a dark blue leather-bound, gilt-lettered first edition of Now We Are Six *(for his sixth birthday), an all-brass geometry set in a mahogany box lined with maroon velvet, one of the first ever microscopes and, much to Mother's horror, a walking stick which hides a sword, although Simon is under strict instructions not to show it to any of his friends. But I happen to know that Simon has disobeyed this instruction. I shall hold this information until a time when it may be useful.*

Dad is more excited for Simon on his birthdays than Simon is.

But when Simon opened the box that contained an early Brownie camera, complete with original film and in perfect working order, no one, not even Dad could have predicted the pleasure that this would bring him

So we can blame Dad. Because that was the day that Simon became a camera bore.

∞

Sadie answers the door covered in dust. She is wearing paint-spattered joggers and one of Simon's shirts. Her hair is scraped back off her face. I hadn't noticed that it had grown long enough to allow her to do this.

'I was up in the attic.'

'Oh. What are you doing?'

Sadie bites her lip and looks down, away from me.

'I'm, er, just sorting stuff, you know. There's baby things that we don't need anymore and things like that, you know.'

It's not like Sadie to be so incoherent.

'How are you?' I ask her.

She bites her thumb nail and slightly raises her eyebrows. I interpret this as meaning, 'not good'.

'Can we not talk about stuff today?'

'Fine. Whatever. I'll just take Hannah and go then, shall I?'

I'm beyond feeling awkward in her presence. However she wants to play it is fine by me.

'Hannah tells me you've got a new boyfriend.'

'She told you that?' I laugh.

'Has she met him? You wouldn't have done that without asking me.'

I won't give her the satisfaction of rising to that bait, so I don't answer.

'I'll go get her things,' says Sadie, backing out of that one.

I go into the living room. Hannah is holding a doll underneath her T-shirt.

'Ssh,' she says to me.

'OK,' I whisper and put my finger to my lips.

'I'm just feeding my baby.'

'Right. Will it take long?'

'No. But then I have to change her nappy and her clothes and put her to bed.'

'Isn't she coming with us?'

'She's going to her nanny. Her nanny is going to look after her while I go out. That's what we always do. And then I'll pick her up in the morning.'

Sadie comes in with Hannah's bag.

She gives her a hug goodbye, then comes with us to the door.

'Aidan is taking us out for lunch, if that's all right with you?'

'Yes, yes of course it is. And I'm sorry. I know you wouldn't—'

'OK. We'll call you later.'

Every time I see or speak to her, she manages to do or say something to alienate herself just that bit further. I have to remind myself that I'm not doing her a favour. I'm spending time with my niece because I enjoy her company, not in order to allow Sadie a life.

1984
Italy! Whose Italy?

The phone rings.

'Hello?'

'I'm coming home.'

I don't say anything for a couple of seconds.

There are no telltale signs. No stifled sobs or strange breathing. Franny sounds completely calm.

'Hattie? Are you there?'

'Yes, yes, of course. What's happened?'

'Can you meet me at the airport?'

'Of course. But Franny . . . are you all right?'

'Considering I've just lost my future?'

'I'll phone you back. Then we can talk. Where are you?'

'I don't know. Some hotel.'

Then she breaks down. It's awful. I keep asking her to let me phone her back. Knowing Franny, she won't have enough money to pay for the hotel room, let alone a long-distance telephone call. But she's right, I can't be concerned about that – not while her life is in tatters. I'm not glad that it's all over, that Fabrizio wouldn't appreciate the sacrifices that Franny had made in order to be with him, that he became sullen, distant, abusive, tried to clip her wings, domesticise her, start to resent her, make her unhappy then finally abandon her in a place far away from all she knew, that she had tried so hard to make her home. But I am glad she's coming back. Somehow it feels wrong to tell her this now. That can wait. Until I see her.

Simon has this photograph album singularly devoted to himself. For the first year of his life there is a picture for every month. Two pictures cover the second and third years. And from then on there is a single portrait for every year of his thirty-nine years.

I find it disorientating. It's like one of those time-lapse films of flowers blooming. Is it possible that he will keep this up for his entire life, so we can watch the flower bloom, then fade and die?

'I think I need a character.'

'Yes. That can work. As long as you get it absolutely right.'

'I'd rather approach it like that. Then it's not actually me that dies a death. I can take the costume and the make-up off and no one will know that that was me up there not managing to make anyone laugh. Oh, my God.'

It's not that difficult, this meeting. But then, I haven't told Luke anything about Aidan.

'I had this dream the other night,' I tell him, 'about Jerry Seinfeld. But he was really fat. You know huge, and he was doing stand-up. Just him and the mike. Not like he does it in the show, but in this vast packed stadium. But no one from the show was there and I kept thinking, "Where are all Jerry's friends?" But there weren't any of them there, except for me – watching him from the wings.'

'Fuck me!' says Luke. 'That's amazing.'

'Is it? Why?'

'Well, he is huge, isn't he? He's the most successful television comedian ever.'

'Is he? Where did you read that? *TV Comics Weekly?*'

It's good to see Luke laugh again. We always did that for each other. But that's all, I think.

'Great dream. God, I wish I'd had that dream.'

'Why?'

'How did you feel in the dream?'

'I don't know. OK. Fine. Happy. Safe.'

'I knew it was right for you to do this.'

'You keep saying that.'

'But this proves it. Seinfeld equals success. A fat Seinfeld equals huge success. You obviously have no subconscious fears about doing this at all. You see yourself being as big as Jerry Seinfeld.'

'Hmm. That would be rather arrogant of me. But I've been thinking about characters. And I wrote this stuff down about a single mother. See what you think.'

I hand Luke three hand-written sheets. He takes them, sits back in his chair and reads. I watch his face intently. It doesn't change expression. He doesn't laugh. He doesn't smile. Nothing on his face moves at all. It takes him about five minutes to read it. When he gets to the end, he re-reads the whole thing again.

I have been sitting there watching him for nearly fifteen minutes before he looks at me.

'It's a start,' he says.

I can't bear it any longer.

'Is it funny?'

'What do you think?'

I grab back the sheets and look through them.

'There's actually only one joke in there,' he says.

'That doesn't mean there's only one laugh though, does it?' I ask him.

'No.'

'Which do you think is the one joke?'

'The bit about the thirteen-year-old boy who's only just discovered that his parents have separated.'

I giggle.

'I like that bit,' I say.

'It's funny. Tell me that joke.'

I look at the paper.

Luke snatches it from me.

'No. Don't read it. Tell me the joke.'

'There's this little boy who— No, that's wrong. Um. This woman decides not to tell her son the truth about— No, that's not going to work either. I can't. It only works in context.'

'Exactly,' says Luke.

'Oh,' I say. This is going to be even harder than I thought.

1993
How many lawyers does it take . . . ?

Dad insists that I see a solicitor. Do I think that Adam won't?

Yes, I do think that Adam won't.

Why?

Because he doesn't bother about things.

I'm not sure that I want to be the first one to go to a solicitor. It makes it all into something else. Something real.

Dad insists. We have a home together. It has to be decided what we do with it.

Dad is right, of course. And he knows just the right solicitor for me to see.

Finally I agree. Particularly after Dad offers to pay the fees.

'Steamed organic carrots and potatoes,' says Kate, handing me one jar. 'And apple and blueberry purée.' She hands me another. 'Are you sure about this?'

'Kate!' Baby Bardolph is sitting on my lap, sucking on a slither of cucumber. Organic, of course.

Kate leans down to her son and places her lips on his cheek. She then appears to suck the life out of him. It's quite frightening the passion with which she kisses him.

'I'll be about an hour. Hour and a half. Two hours maximum.'

'It's fine. Honestly. Just go. Be fabulous. Get the job.'

'God. Suppose I do get it. What do I do?'

'We'll work it out.'

She drops her mobile into her bag.

'You will call me?'

'No, I won't.'

'I've not left him for this long before.'

'Seriously?'

'Of course not. If he wants me—'

'He will want you. You're his mother. But he'll know that I'm here to look after him. And when you get back, he'll be all the more pleased to see you. And we'll have had a good time together. Won't we?' I bounce BB on my lap, who gurgles in response. 'See?'

'Yeah. I'm going. This is me walking out of the door. Leaving my home without my baby. Oh God, I can't do it.'

'Yes, you can. Go. We'll be here.'

I am pushing her towards the front door. She's almost out of the door, but she can't leave without one final cuddle. BB is totally confused. He is starting to get distressed.

'I can't leave now. Not while he's like this.' She puts her bag on the floor and takes BB from my arms, who is now so confused that he lets rip an enormous yell.

'I'll have to calm him down. I'll just give him a bit of bosom. And then I'll go. Could you phone them for me and tell them I'll be a bit late?'

1987
I'd like to sleep for ever

Kate is still unconscious. Every so often she turns, says, 'Simon?' then drifts off again into her artificial sleep.

But Simon isn't here. I am.

Every so often a nurse comes in and says, 'Won't be long now. She'll wake soon. Let me know when she does,' and goes out again.

Kate is taking a long time to come round and they need the bed.

The nurse comes in again.

'She shouldn't still be out. The anaesthetic normally lasts less than half an hour.'

'But she is all right, isn't she?' I ask.

The nurse checks her pulse, gently shakes her and calls her name. Kate opens her eyes then closes them again.

'Yes, she's all right,' says the nurse and goes.

My guess is that Kate doesn't want to wake up.

1987
How do you think she is?

He is waiting for me outside the stage door.

'How is she?' he asks.

I don't know how to treat him. He's my brother and I love him. But she's my best friend and I love her too. I wish he hadn't come. I'm exhausted and emotionally wrought from the rehearsals and the first night and the first-night party. I've just had the deflating experience of a second-night performance. And I'm tired of thinking I should play Simon's conscience.

I shrug my shoulders.

'Stupid question,' I say.

1989
It was only a joke

'What was her name?'

Simon is ignoring me.

'Simon, you remember. She had that really whiny voice and she'd ring up and whine, "Is Simon there?" Sometimes I'd tell her she had the wrong number.'

'What? You never told me that before.'

'Oops. Haven't I? Oh, so now you know.'

'How many other people did you do that to?'

'None. Just her. What was her name?'

'Louise.'

'Of course. How could I forget? Loopy Lou!'

'I didn't know you called her that.'

'You two did live in the same house, didn't you?' asks Sadie. 'I'm glad you're telling me all this, Hattie. I'd never have got all this information about Simon's past out of him.'

Simon flings his left arm around Sadie's neck and pulls her sideways towards his side of the sofa.

'It's not my past that matters,' he says. 'Only my very thrilling present and my much to look forward to future.'

Sadie melts against him. He kisses the top of her head. With her eyes closed to receive the kiss, she moves her left thumb over the empty fourth finger of the same hand. It is a tiny movement but a huge gesture. And it shocks me. I find myself doing the same, but my thumb bumps into a curved gold band that sits nestled into another gold band which has embedded in it a one-carat diamond. It's a heavy combination. How can I forget that they are there? I look over to the other armchair. Adam is sitting in it. I had forgotten he was there too. He winks at me, takes a long drag on his cigarette and disappears back inside himself. Simon and Sadie are still enjoying their cuddle. I feel terribly alone.

'Excuse me, do you mind if I ask you a question?'

Franny and I turn away from the antique stall where she is just getting ready to part with £15 for a small

Victorian jug, and towards a young girl holding a notebook. Behind her is a man with a serious-looking camera.

'I work for *Woman's Weekly*, and we're doing a piece on memorable first kisses. Would you like to tell us about yours?'

Franny and I look at each other and smile.

'What's he doing?' Franny asks, indicating the photographer.

'If you agree we'll take your photo. There's no guarantee we'll use you, though.'

Franny and I say nothing.

'Please,' she says. 'I've only got to get two more, then I can go home.'

How can we refuse?

She turns to Franny.

'What's your name? You can make one up if you like.'

'Francesca di Riccio.'

'Are you Italian?'

Franny smiles enigmatically.

'I have been,' she says.

'So tell me about a memorable first kiss.'

'It's difficult to single one out.' Franny pauses to think. 'You go,' she says to me, 'while I think about it.'

All I can think about is Tom. How we were drawn to each other like magnets; how our lips travelled towards each other in slow motion so that the anticipation of the pleasure in their meeting multiplied with each millisecond of their journey; how I lost consciousness for a tiny moment when they did finally meet and how no other first kiss has come anywhere near.

I try to find the words to express this. It comes out

all wrong. The journalist smiles and takes notes, but it makes no sense. Well, that's her job. She quickly moves back to Franny.

1983
I have this thing about Abstract Expressionism

I like this job. It makes me feel like I'm in the right place at the right time. Mostly, I like the people who visit Art exhibitions. All I am doing is taking their money and handing them tickets, but I feel a kindred spirit as I press the button and tear off the small rectangular, pink (regular price), green (concessions), or blue (Friends of The Tate discount) passports into another world.

I have a favourite painting. It's called Untitled. *It takes up a whole wall. This is a big exhibition.*

In the morning when I arrive, it says to me, 'Good morning. Welcome.'

When I leave and go to say goodbye, it says, 'See you tomorrow. I'll be here.'

I like to know that.

And when I sit in front of it during a coffee break, its vast blueness and red earth stripe comfort me.

'We're all in this together,' it says.

1983
Oh, it's you

We stop selling tickets about thirty minutes before we close. Anyone who arrives during that time usually gets in for free.

Fifteen minutes to go, I am vaguely distracted by a mediocre book when I become aware of someone standing in front of the counter. I look up. It's Tom. I always forget how small he is.

'I'm afraid we're about to close,' I say.

Not, 'Hello. How are you? It's been ages. What the fuck are you doing here, you bastard?'

'I haven't come to see the exhibition. I've come to see you.'

I look at him.

He smiles that smile.

I hate him.

1980
And I fell for it

Almost everybody has gone. I am sitting on a chair in the kitchen amongst the party remains. Tom is on the floor, leaning against me. I am stroking his hair.

Grace comes in, takes one look at us and says, 'Oh, Christ,' and goes out again.

'I never wanted to be an actor,' he says. 'I wanted to be a fireman.'

1979
Who's that man?

After Simon leaves University and before he moves into the flat, he decides to travel for the Summer. His student card is still valid, so he buys one of those go-wherever-you-want-to-in-Europe-by-train tickets. I want a holiday too, so Simon and I arrange to meet up in Athens.

I hate Athens. It's hot, dusty, windy and noisy.

Carrying our well-thumbed copies of The Magus *we head for Spetses, the scene of the crime. We are not alone in our pilgrimage. The clean, calm beaches of Spetses are littered with undernourished pasty students deeply engrossed in the black paperback with its distinctive orange and white lettering on the spine.*

So when I spot a well-built, tanned, dark-haired, long-eyelashed beauty concentrating on a library edition of volume VII of Remembrance of Things Past, *I am immediately intrigued.*

1979
Hello stranger (2)

'It's him. There he is.'

I nudge Simon and point towards the well-built, tanned, dark-haired, long-eyelashed beauty sitting by himself at a café. He is not reading. Or drinking. Just sitting.

'Looks the melancholy type to me.'

'You sound just like Dad sometimes.'

'Well, he does. Look at him – all broody and mysterious.'

'Do you think so?' *I am even more intrigued.*

Simon takes out his camera and takes half a dozen shots of him.

'Simon!'

'Are you going to talk to him?'

'I think that might be a bit much. Perhaps I'll start with a smile.

Then, when we've spent a couple of days smiling at each other, we can work up towards a greeting, then after a few days of that we may then be ready for a conversation.'

But I am talking to no one because to my horror Simon has joined the beauty at his table and is introducing himself. They both look over at me and smile. The beauty has pale blue eyes and straight white teeth. Simon beckons.

Since when did Simon become my procurer?

'He's not really dead. He's just pretending. Even though he knows it's Simba, he doesn't wake up because he's playing a trick on him.'

'No, darling. Hard as it may be for you to accept, he is actually dead. That's the whole point of the film. He is the Lion King, not his father. Well, that's not true, they both are.' I shut up. I'm just confusing the poor child.

Hannah screams at me, 'HE'S NOT DEAD!'

'No, he is.'

'But we see him at the end.'

'You don't. That's Simba grown up.'

'No it's not. It's the Daddy. And the Mummy and the Daddy have another baby.'

'No. That's Simba's baby.'

'No it's not. He didn't get married. So how can he be having a baby?'

'Umm. You can. You don't have to be married to have a baby.'

Hannah is silent. For ages.

'Are my Mummy and Daddy married?' she finally asks.

∞

'I need to go to the bank,' says Dad. 'Hattie, do you want to come?'

I've been silently fuming about an article in the *Daily Mail*, so I put down the paper and say, 'Yes, OK.'

We leave Mother looking perplexed and feeling abandoned.

In the car Dad says to me, 'Simon and Sadie aren't living together, are they?'

'No. No they're not.'

Dad says nothing.

'How long have you known?' I ask him.

'We may be your parents, but we're not stupid.'

'Does Mother know?'

Dad is silent.

I laugh.

'She doesn't, does she? The whole thing is ridiculous. How do you know? She might know and just isn't saying anything to you, like you've not said anything to her.'

'She'd be terribly hurt.'

'I know. It would probably bring on some dreadful disease that no one will be able to diagnose.'

'Hattie! Your mother, unfortunately, does not enjoy good health.'

'Absolutely. You've hit the nail on the head. Mother only enjoys bad health. She's only happy if there's something wrong with her.'

I look at him. It can't be easy living with Mother. I only had eighteen years of it before I got out. But Dad. Poor Dad. He's in it for the duration.

'I think this whole secrecy thing is crazy. And I've told Simon. But he's so obstinate. He's so convinced that him and Sadie will work it out.'

'What do you think?'

'I don't think they will,' I say slowly.

I surprise myself by having a major panic attack simply because I had not heard from Aidan at the time he said he would call.

Feelings of hatred for Adam always resurface at times like these and I begin to feel like I am not as much over the whole damn thing as I think I am. This is because at times like these I cannot draw a line between levels of betrayal; seven years of continually being lied to, cheated on and betrayed has an equal status with a phone call that comes ninety minutes late.

Perhaps I should join an Art class and learn how to paint landscapes (watercolours, I think) then I will at least learn something about perspective.

Even worse – I can't divulge any of this to Aidan as I don't want him to feel responsible for how I react to situations, especially if my reaction is extreme.

So who am I? I'm starting to suffer an identity crisis. Am I the funny, talented, sexy woman that Aidan is so obviously drawn to? Or is the real me the five-year-old inside (OK, a slightly mature five-year-old who has at least learned only to have tantrums when alone and unwatched) who still is in desperate need of unconditional love?

Maybe I would have had a better life as a dog, then I would be truly, madly barking, but I think of the fate of Harvey and realise canine identity is no guarantee of enduring security.

Why didn't Mother ever tell me how hard all this would be? Mainly, I suspect, because Mother never found out.

Dad wouldn't let her.

Lucky Mother.

Chapter Ten

In which our heroine discovers the truth about her marriage, helps her brother and best friend through a difficult time, becomes enchanted and loses a bet

The beginning of Summer brings the perennial problem of excess body hair; how much to remove, when to remove it and the method of removal keeps North London's phone lines buzzing for several weeks. Of course, if I did not have a regular lover to display naked flesh to, then the problem would not be quite so severe. I simply cannot wait the four weeks between sugarings advised to me by the 'really-should-be-living-in-LA-Rita' of my local beauty salon. If

I were to do this, I could not possibly inflict the sight of down-covered legs on Aidan and we would have to only have sex in the dark and refrain from communal baths. This would be a great shame and necessarily place a strain on the relationship. Perhaps they're not as bad as I think they are; I mean, we're not exactly talking Robin Williams here. No. Any body hair is too much body hair, for me.

The only thing to do is risk the wrath of Rita and reach for the razor. There is now a huge marketing opportunity in lady's shaving so I spend far too long in the Chemist trying to decide between Gillette Lady's Shaving Gel with added aloe vera, and Wilkinson Sword Lady's Shaving Gel with camomile. I finally decide on Gillette as the can is green as opposed to pink and I do try to steer well away from anything pink in the bathroom lest anyone should think I grew up in the provinces.

Summer also brings the anticipation of my birthday and its accompanying emotional exhaustion. Around the start of June I always used to issue a present list to Adam who would circulate it around his family and therefore I would generally receive wanted, needed presents that may have not had much thought put into them but certainly got appreciated and used.

Now times have changed, but I really must cease to judge my friends by the presents they buy. Presents don't always articulate the level of importance you have in the donator's life, but it is sometimes hard for me to accept otherwise.

Fuck it! I'll come out on this one. Birthdays *are* a test.

Nothing like putting pressure on myself or my friends, is there?

But if I got bought anything that had anything to do with hair removal, I certainly would take offence and have to seriously reconsider the position of the giver in my life.

1979
'. . . as true a lover as ever sighed upon a midnight pillow'

I'm doubly cross with Simon. Firstly, because he never spoke to me about his feelings for Kate. Never told me he fancied her, liked her, was interested in her, wanted to get to know her. And secondly, because he never actually told me what Kate told me, that is that it had happened. They are together and both of them have fallen in love.

All this is happening right under my nose. I mean, we all live together. So in a sense I don't need to be told anything. I can see what's going on.

Kate is so happy. She really enjoys being in love. She throws herself into the wonderfulness of it and lifts everyone around her in her enhanced enthusiasm for life, work and people. She smiles, she laughs. We all benefit from Kate's happiness. She always was talented – she has that spark, that little extra quality that you need to succeed and being in love only increases her abilities. We are reaching the end of our first year and are rehearsing As You Like It to tour around the parks during the Summer. Kate is Rosalind. She is magnificent.

Simon is overawed by Kate. He obviously adores her. But he cannot reconcile himself with the notion that he is responsible for the truly wonderful Kate that has emerged — that it is her feelings for him that have released such joy into her life.

I know this because he told me so as we drank a bottle of wine together one night nearly six weeks after Kate moved into his room.

'There are three men around you.'

'Oh. Three?'

'No. I'm wrong. There are five.'

'Five?'

'One of them is a fire sign. That's not good for you. Do you know who I mean?'

'Which are the fire signs?'

'I don't know.'

No, of course she doesn't — she's a psychic not an astrologer.

'Oh, I know,' I say. 'Sagittarius. That's a fire sign. But I don't know any Sagittarians. Except Rufus. And he's not yet two. You don't mean him, do you?'

She doesn't answer. Every so often she appears to remove herself and slightly cocks her head to one side. Her pupils move to the corners of her eyes. This, I learn, is when she is listening to her voices.

'This Fire sign man. He's older than you. Cocky. Bit of a know-all. But he's no match for you. He knows that. It's not good.'

I suddenly realise I don't know when Aidan's birthday is, but do know that Aidan is Old Irish for 'fire'. Oh fuck.

'Can you tell me anything else about him?'

'I see phones. He likes to talk on the phone. He does a lot of business on the phone.'

I sink back in my chair. Who doesn't do a lot of business on the phone?

'There's laughter around him. Money and laughter. That's an odd mixture. He makes his money out of laughter, doesn't he?'

Shit! Why did I come?

'I think I know who you mean,' I say.

'He's not a bad man. A little devious, perhaps. Not a liar. He's good. But not good enough for you. And he knows that. He's in awe of your power. He knows he can't match it. He's not the man for you.'

Personally I don't think psychics should tell you things like that.

'So what about the other four?' I ask, holding back the tears.

1966
'A script has to make sense and life doesn't'

My favourite place for watching the Sunday afternoon movie is lying on the floor on my side, underneath the coffee table. Dad sits in his reclining armchair, smoking his pipe, either reading the Sunday papers or falling asleep and dreaming out loud about his war experiences, or occasionally he'll look at the television and make some comment like, 'He's not in this for nothing.' Or, 'She's Jewish.' Or, 'What's his name? He's very well known but I can't think of his name.'

Mother bangs about in the kitchen, letting us all know how she feels about clearing up Sunday lunch unaided.

And Simon sits perched on the edge of the sofa intently watching the screen, taking in as much of what is happening as possible.

While I gasp, stunned as a transformed Bette Davis walks down the aeroplane steps, slim, lipsticked and beautifully dressed, Simon comments on camera angles and lighting.

While I thrall over how Rita Hayworth's dress remains still while she slinks around inside it and doesn't reveal any more of her than the Hays Code would allow, even when she flips that magnificent head of hair over and over, Simon lectures on the one-take scene.

And while I giggle with delight as the leopard follows Cary Grant around, Simon tells us about early split-screen techniques.

And this is how we learn to love the movies.

'*It's a Wonderful Life, Some Like It Hot, Raging Bull, Three Colours Red, The Sound of Music—*'

'You're not serious. *The Sound of Music?*'

'How many is that?'

'Five.' Aidan is laughing.

I continue.

'*Rebecca, Woman of the Year, Singing in the Rain, Schindler's List* and *Terminator 2.*'

Aidan has not stopped laughing.

'That's an interesting list. I wonder what an analyst would make of someone who had *The Sound of Music* and *Terminator 2* on their top ten favourite movie list.'

'I think they'd think, "There's someone who understands what makes a movie a good movie." So? Tell me yours.'

'*Seven Samurai, High Plains Drifter, The Ladykillers, Hiroshima, Mon Amour, Laura, On the Waterfront, Vertigo, The Roaring Twenties, Five Easy Pieces* and *Bambi.*'

'Nice list. Funny. Neither of us had any Woody Allens.'

'That's because he deserves a best movie list all of his own.'

'That's what Simon and I have always thought!' I'm very impressed by all this, but to tell Aidan would appear patronising. 'You must meet Simon.'

'I'd love to.'

He says it so quickly it comes out as almost a reprimand to me for not having suggested it sooner.

'OK. Right.'

'So, when?'

Is he being a bit pushy about this?

'I don't know. Maybe I'll do a dinner and maybe Kate could come too.'

'That sounds good. How are things between Kate and Simon?'

I suddenly feel terribly disloyal discussing this with Aidan.

'I'm not sure really,' is all I'm prepared to say.

It has become almost impossible to prevent the flow from my eyes. But she's obviously used to this and tactfully ignores it.

'You will have a child,' she tells me. 'But first you must sort out the violence in your life.'

1980
It's not supposed to be like this

'Hattie. Hattie. Let me in. Hattie.'

Tom is in the street. I am two floors up, sitting on the floor leaning against the wall underneath the window with my knees up against my chest. The lights are off. The room is lit only by the glow of a street lamp two doors down.

Tom does not believe that I am not here. But he has been shouting for so long now that it would be worse to let him in and suffer the recriminations for not answering the door sooner, than to let him continue humiliating himself.

The phone rings. The shouting stops. If he can hear the phone he can hear me answer it. I must stay where I am. The phone stops. Tom is silent. I dare not attempt to look out of the window and risk him seeing me.

I'm tired; I need to be in my bed but I'm convinced that he may hear every movement that I make. I have to stay put.

It's been quiet for fifteen minutes now.

I'll crawl up to my bedroom.

I'm out of the lounge now, passing the front door on my way upstairs. The front door intercom buzzes. It sounds like a normal person. Not Tom's just-too-long usual ring. But I won't fall for that one.

I am right not to. Almost immediately the buzzer sounds again. Longer this time. Then again. Even longer. The next buzz seems like it will never end. But I will not let him in.

I'm in the bedroom now. I don't take off my clothes but slide under the covers and hope that the noises will stop; hope that Tom will stop; hope that life will stop. Because this is no way to live it.

1987
Breaking up is hard to do

I've never seen Simon like this before. He has his moods – he's a Capricorn. But this. This is something else.

For about a week now he has been ringing me at least twice a day, then staying silent while I try to guess what he wants to say. When we finally arrange to meet, I am shocked by his appearance, unwashed, unshaved, unkempt.

'I can't do it. I just can't do it. I don't even know why. I just know I can't.'

He is only too aware of my split loyalties. He has to play safe.

'I don't know what to say,' I tell him.

'Tell me what I should do?'

'And what good would that do?'

He doesn't answer.

'Kate knows how you feel, doesn't she?' *(As if I don't know the answer to this!)*

'I think so. Obviously we've talked about nothing else. She wants it, but she wants me too. And I've as good as told her she can't have both.'

'Simon! That's horrible.'

'What's horrible is . . . what is tormenting me . . . is why.'

'It's scary . . . fatherhood. All that responsibility. It's grown up stuff. Real life. It's like fun time's over, now this is the hard bit. Of course you feel like that.'

'I honestly, truly don't feel ready for this.'

'And Kate thinks it's about her, not the baby.'

'She said that?'

'Not exactly. But I know that's what I'd think. You don't love her enough for her to have your baby.'

Simon's eyes cloud over. He hides them behind his hands. He sits like that for a couple of minutes. Then I take one of his hands and hold it in mine.

'It's been such a good time. The best time,' he says.

'But things change. Time to move on.'

'I don't want to grow old with her. I want us to have always been young together.'

'Jesus, you're full of shit sometimes.' I drop his hand. 'You're right – you're not ready.'

'Thank God for you,' says Simon, wiping his eyes with the back of his hand and almost managing a smile.

'Yeah,' I say, 'someone's got to point out to you the difference between real life and the movies. Who do you think you are, bleedin' Heathcliff?'

'If she decides to go ahead—'

'I don't think she will.'

Simon looks shocked.

'Be practical, for goodness' sake.'

'I know, yes, you're right.'

'This is going to break you up.'

'I know.'

'It will be harder for her than for you.'

'Yeah, I know.'

'God, I hope you know what you're doing.'

'Of course I don't.' Simon practically screams at me.

I can't help him.

'Did I tell you, the show's transferring. We're doing a fill-in *because of some ghastly thing that closed early. We've got the Wyndham's for four weeks.'*

Simon looks at me as if he doesn't understand what I'm saying.

'The West End,' I tell him. 'My West End debut.'

He smiles.

'That's wonderful.'

'Yeah.' I shrug my shoulders. 'Isn't it.'

1987
Tears wash the eyes so that one can see better

It does not seem possible that anyone can cry this much. As I hold Kate while she sobs, I can feel her heart breaking. Her movements are violent. She wants every part of her to feel the pain. It's as if she wants to break up her body. She has no use for it anymore. That little bit of her, and that little bit of Simon that would have been with her for ever, is gone. Dead. Killed. And she did it. She made that happen.

She scribbles a note and gives it to me, asking me to keep it safe.

The front of the folded sheet says, 'To Simon'. But he will never see it. I'll know, she says, when to give it back to her. Kate's excessively large writing is scrawled diagonally across the roughly torn paper saying: 'IOU One Life'.

1993
Earthquake in Highgate Woods

'How long have you known her?' I ask.

'How long do you think?'

'Five years,' I say, for no particular reason.

'Yes,' says Adam.

I look around. People, families are sitting at tables laughing, drinking, eating. Children are running around. Dogs are barking.

Did no one notice the deafening noise as the crack appeared in the surface of the planet?

I am seated at the epicentre of an earthquake.

No, I'm not.

It's only the sound of my past shattering into tiny pieces.

∞

'It feels different, you know. Oh, I can't explain.'

'I know what's happening.' Franny has an unmistake-able glint in her eye.

'What?' I ask her. 'And stop smiling like that.'

But she can't. Franny just cannot stop smiling.

'Stop it,' I say. But it's infectious. I, too, am smil-ing now.

'It's because you're not having sex—'

'Yes we are. We had sex last night. And this morning. Don't you love that early morning sleepy sex?'

'No you're not. You're making love.'

I stop smiling. I sit perfectly still. I need to think about this one.

'Oh.'

Franny's smile turns into a giggle. Franny has the most marvellous giggle. It is pure innocent delight. She giggles like a baby having its tummy tickled.

'Don't look so serious.'

'But it is serious. I've never made love in my life.'

'Yes you have. Last night and this morning.'

'Do you? Of course you do. You always have done.'

'Not always. But I will admit that I'm much better at it than you. You always hide behind having sex. It keeps the distance. You need distance. Let's face it, you're a complete commitment-phobe.'

'How can you say that?'

'Well, looks like things are on the change for you.'

'Oh God. Really? Shit. I know I don't fall in love the same way you do. No one falls in love the same way you do. Or as often. No, I can't. Anyway, Psychic Stella told me not to.'

'Did you find out when Aidan's birthday was?'

'Yes. 31 August.'

'That's makes him Virgo. That's not a Fire sign.'

'Isn't it? Are you sure?'

'Yes it's an Earth sign. Perfect complement to a flighty Air sign like you.'

'Really? So she wasn't talking about Aidan?'

'Doesn't look like it.'

'But all that stuff about money and laughter?'

'What about Luke? What star sign is he?'

'I don't know. You know I only know the barest minimum about these things. His birthday was March. Just before I met him.'

'End or beginning?'

'End.'

'Aries. Definitely a fire sign.'

'So all that stuff was about Luke, not about Aidan?'

I feel really stupid. For the past week or so I've played it down with Aidan, finding reasons to get irritable with him, raising my standards to make him unacceptable, looking around for fanciable men – basically protecting myself.

'What's interesting,' says Franny, 'is that you wanted to believe her. You didn't want it to work out with Aidan. Running away again, see?'

'Hmmmm.'

'Go for it.'

'I'm not doing it alone. If we jump in, we jump in together, holding hands. Like Meg Ryan and Tom Hanks in *Joe versus the Volcano*.'

Franny leans over to hug me.

'Just fucking do it,' she says.

1988
Careering from career to career

Simon's got that lost look again. What is it about him? He's really tried hard this last year. It's not been easy. He's made major life-changing decisions. He's broken up with Kate, moved home, left his job and turned thirty. Actually, he turned thirty first. An early mid-life crisis? Perhaps not. All men have crises at thirty. It's just that some of them have them later on as well.

Since leaving his job with the Civil Service he's been floating around a bit. Now he's come up with this idea of starting a sandwich-making business. He tries it and it seems to be doing very well. He makes the sandwiches in his kitchen then travels down to the city and lugs this huge basket around those offices that will let him. Every day he runs out and every day he makes even more. So he gets some help.

Toby helps him for a while, but this does not work out. It's evidently demeaning for a man of Toby's talents to be touting sandwiches around. Anyway, he spends far too much time chatting up the city boys, trying to make them laugh with theatrical tales. Any work that isn't performing eventually brings on one of Toby's depressions. So he stops selling sandwiches.

Simon is doing so well he thinks about opening a shop. He looks around for premises in the city, but fortunately before he can settle on anything Black Monday happens and the word goes out that the city's workforce is about to halve. It no longer seems such a good place to be selling sandwiches.

So Simon has that look about him again. I tell him this may be a good time to take the plunge with his photography. Instead of it being a pocket money-making hobby, why not try it as a career?

Simon thinks about it, but is too worried that if he depended on it to make a living he would eventually have to compromise his artistic integrity.

I tell him, bollocks.

He's already done several shoots of portraits for me and other actors; he's done stills for a couple of the big shows and the more people he meets, the more contacts he makes. People start recommending him for work; eventually he does nothing else all day and hey, he's got a career.

Simon remains unconvinced, but tells me to severely reprimand him if I ever find out he's off to do a wedding.

1974
Could it be for ever?

Of course, Simon thinks it's highly amusing. Mother, amazingly, understands that it is part of growing up and Dad indulges me by giving me extra pocket money so that I can fill my second scrapbook with pictures of David Cassidy cut out from any magazine I can find that contains them.

You see Margie and I have a bet on. We are in competition to obtain the most photographs of our teen idol – or 'true love' in my case.

'Welcome to the real world,' sneers Simon as The Lady of Shallot, Narcissus and the Nymphs *and my beloved* Chatterton *are temporarily removed from my walls and replaced by a grinning boy/man with layered brown locks, open shirts and a fine line in hipster flared jeans.*

No one, on pain of death, is allowed to talk to me, ask me a question or demand anything off me for twenty-five minutes on a Saturday afternoon while I watch 'The Partridge Family'. Nothing short of impending nuclear devastation will shift me. Actually, not even that. The four-minute warning would at least allow me four glorious minutes of delectable David. And I would die happy.

I know he thinks about me. It's obvious. Because he knows how I feel. I can tell by the way he looks at me. And there are too many coincidences. I mean, every time I think about him I only have to open my eyes and I see him. He is everywhere. I devote a whole page of my scrapbook to a full-length portrait which I decorate with hearts. Lots of tiny hearts that make up one big heart that frames my love.

And how's this for a coincidence? I stay in bed one day, because I'm not feeling well (lovesick) and I really should be at school, and I think to myself, if I listen to Radio One all day they're bound to play 'Could It Be For Ever' at some point. And what do you know? At about eleven o'clock, they do! Margie is furious when I tell her that one and accuses me of faking illness so that I could listen to the radio, which, of course, I vehemently deny.

As a result of this, Margie ups her campaign and employs the assistance of her American cousin, who sends over from the States sackloads of David Cassidy stuff, enrols her in the David Cassidy US Fan Club and promises her tickets to view the filming of 'The Partridge Family' if she ever gets over to LA.

I am disarmed. I concede defeat and am forced to hand over my most precious possession, the subject of the bet, a pair of David's actual sunglasses that he wore in the episode of 'The Partridge Family' where the kids suspect Mom of having a new boyfriend, so they follow her around, in disguise. And these very glasses were part of David's disguise and I won them in a competition in Jackie. The only time I ever won anything in my life. And now I must be without them. David will never forgive me. My feelings for him can never be the same.

Not now that my love is clouded by shame and guilt.

I wish I'd never made the stupid bet.

'All's fair in love and stupid bets,' says Simon, not reassuring me at all.

It's not long before the posters begin to change again. The first new addition being Millais' Ophelia. Far more enduring than the fickleness of teenage adoration.

Luke asks me to come to a comedy workshop he's running.

It's completely terrifying. The atmosphere in the room is highly charged. There's a lot of anger here. I think that's sad and wrong. Most of these people are confusing stand-up comedy with Speaker's Corner. It's not a licence to rant against the world's injustices. But try telling them that. Because they think they know differently. They all want to be Lenny Bruce. Or Ben Elton. Too late. It's already been done.

I don't contribute much to the day. I feel completely out of my depth.

Besides, I feel completely inhibited by the shock appearance of a figure from my past.

Bernice.

Her flaming red hair has been severed into a neat bob and there is a new addition of scarlet lips and matching talons. She still chain smokes. And she still has the same smell. Simon used to call it 'Mad' – like it was the actual name of a scent you could buy. I know she won't recognise me without prompting. I was fourteen when we last had any contact. I realise now that she is probably only six or seven years older than me. But when you're fourteen, the difference is huge. It's the difference between being a child and an adult.

1974
I know that smell

Dad rings the bell. We wait. Dad rings the bell again. We wait some more.

I don't want to be here. I'm skulking around at the bottom of the steps that lead up to the front door. Dad made me come with him because he said I needed to get out of the house. It wasn't healthy to sleep until midday, not get dressed until three and just lie around watching the television. So he made me come with him to check out some problem at one of his flats. But it doesn't look like the tenants are at home.

He rings the bell for a third time. A short, quick buzz allows him to push open the front door.

'Hattie?' he says.

I walk slowly up the steps and he lets me enter in front of him. The hallway is dark. I press a time switch. Nothing. Dad gets out his notebook and writes a note to change the bulb. We climb the stairs to the first floor.

I've not been to this house before. Dad is always taking me to houses that I've never been to before. I have no idea how many he owns or where they all are. And Dad gets depressed that I show no interest in the business.

He knocks on the door of Flat 3.

'What's that smell?' he asks not really to me, more to the smell itself.

I know that smell because I've smelt it in Kensington Market.

'Patchouli,' I tell him.

'Bless you,' he says.

'Ha ha,' I say.

As the door opens the smell punches us in the guts and we both reel backwards slightly.

Standing in the doorway is a small, white-skinned, bony girl. Unbrushed auburn locks fall straight over her face down to her waist. She is tiny. A long, maroon, crushed-velvet tent hangs loosely over her minute frame and silver bells hanging from a silver ankle chain chime discordantly as she shuffles uncomfortably on the doorstep.

'Hello, Bernice,' says Dad.

Bernice smiles, sort of. Well, she changes the shape of what little of her mouth we can see behind the curtain of hair. I presume it is supposed to be a smile.

'Can we come in?' asks Dad ever so nicely.

Bernice says nothing, just moves aside to let us pass.

'This is my daughter, Hattie,' he says to her.

'Hi,' I say.

Bernice does that thing with her mouth again.

Inside the flat, the smell of patchouli is overpowered by several other smells, incense, marijuana and cat litter being the most dominant.

Dad recognises the smell of cat litter.

'Have you found homes for the kittens yet?' he asks ever so nicely.

Bernice speaks for the first time, a slow quiet soft Irish voice.

'I'm still looking.'

'We did agree that you could only have the flat on condition you found homes for the cats.'

'Yes, I know.'

'It's been six weeks.'

'Yes I know, but I've had a lot on – looking for a job and everything.'

'Oh, good. Have you found anything?' asks Dad.

'Something,' she answers. 'It's not ideal. But it will do for now.'

Dad doesn't pursue the issue.

We are still in the hallway of the flat. She moves into a large room that I presume is the living room. Black cheesecloth hangs over the windows, tie-dyed cushions are scattered over the carpet, bells and coloured ribbons and crystals on strings hang all over the room. In the centre of the mantelpiece sits an enormous crystal ball.

Dad looks around.

'Well, you've certainly made it your own,' he says, falsely smiling.

Suddenly a kitten leaps out from under the sofa and lands, claws first, on Dad's shoulder.

Dad stays perfectly still, not really sure what has just happened.

Bernice laughs. A glorious rich peat-bog of a laugh which sounds like leprechauns and fiddles and emerald green grass.

'Oisin,' she says, gently lifting the cat-parrot from Dad's jacket, 'that was very naughty. I'm so sorry, Mr Gordon.' She takes the cat out of the room and reappears a few seconds later.

The incident appears to have softened Bernice's mood. She asks us to sit down, offers us herbal teas. (Of what strange drink is she talking?) She asks for my help in finding homes for the three kittens. Surely some of my schoolfriends may be interested? I say I'll ask around.

Then she and Dad disappear while she shows him the leaking bathroom tap and the cracked tiles and the damp in the kitchen.

While they are gone I settle myself on one of the floor cushions and breathe in the pungent scent that is the excuse for air in this room. I lie back and close my eyes. I start to hear sitar music and begin to feel very very warm. I open my eyes. Standing in front of me, just looking at me, is a long thin man, with long hair and a small goatee beard. He wears an open cheesecloth shirt that reveals thin wisps of chest hair that fall neatly into a line which marches down his stomach then disappears behind his thick leather, silver-buckled belt that is doing its best to hold up his very loose jeans. His feet are bare.

'Jesus,' I say, then laugh because that is exactly who he looks like. 'You gave me a fright.'

'You've got a great face,' he says.

I sit up.

'No really,' he continues. 'It's a very lucky face.'

I'm not sure what he means, or who he is for that matter.

'I'm Glyn,' he says because he can read my mind.

'Do you live here too?' I ask.

Glyn smiles.

'Mostly,' he replies.

Then Dad and Bernice come back. Dad has evidently met Glyn before. They shake hands and do 'how-are-yous'.

'I was telling your daughter she has a lucky face,' Glyn tells Dad, to my embarrassment.

Dad smiles proudly. Since when did he listen to hippy talk?

'It will bring her fame,' he says.

'You should listen to Glyn,' says Dad. 'He knows about fame.'

'Are you famous?' I ask him and everyone laughs.

'Only a bit,' he tells me.

'What do you do?'

'Oh, I'm an actor,' he says, as if I meet one every day.

'Are you too?' I ask Bernice.

'Not yet,' she replies.

As we go, Bernice makes me promise to come and see her.

'You can come over whenever you like,' she says. 'Please?'

'Ok,' I say. 'I will.'

Fame. Yes please. I think. Perhaps I'm wrong, but as far as I can make out anyone who says they did not enter the acting profession in order to become famous is very probably lying.

So far the benefits of fame have completely eluded me, or deluded me. The Fame Fairy has visited those close to me. Kate was well sprinkled with fame dust, but sweet Kate, in her sickeningly unfazed way, walked away with an Emmy nomination and a BAFTA award, refusing to sit at home despairing over whether that would be her finest hour. It was and that's just how she wanted it.

Dear Kate lived up to her potential then deliberately failed to live up to her promise. Good for her.

As far as Toby is concerned, fame is the one and only spur. This must be the reason why Toby has to make his presence felt everywhere he goes. Even a trip to the post office will result in the counter staff remembering Toby's visit and, in all likelihood, vowing to take their tea break just in time for his next one. Poor Toby. He's stuck in the belief that people will only remember you if you shout at them and accuse them of incompetence and has forgotten that these may well be the very same people he needs to keep him at the top of wherever it is he is trying to get to. Someone must have told him that the world owes him a living and he's still trying to find out where to cash the cheque.

Grace was the first one to fall and the first one to understand the multi-meanings of fame. She settled for gaining the elusive Equity card by belting out torch songs in Working Men's Clubs, then giving up the whole idea and training as a Youth Worker instead. Clever Grace still kept on her agent, so she occasionally did the odd advert, earned thousands, then went back to her dysfunctional teenagers with renewed street cred and enhanced authority. She had fame where she needed it.

I'm convinced that, apart from the blood bond, Simon and I both share a desire for, if not Fame, then some kind of public recognition – which speaks volumes about a lack of something huge in childhood. Simon is not likely to find it in his present role as a commissioning editor for a small speciality press, but he will never give up his photography. The creative drive and desire for recognition are evidently inextricably linked.

I once heard a theory that all left-handed people are twin survivors – the lost twin dying possibly only days after conception. Apparently there are more of these pregnancies than anyone imagines. My own theory is that all creative people are twin survivors as the creative urge is about searching, searching, searching. Unfortunately the theory cannot be proved without extensive lifetime research. And who would care about the answer anyway?

However, if I could prove it, it would guarantee instant Fame.

Fame. What would I do with it if I had it?

Chapter Eleven

In which our heroine has the Levys over for dinner, sees the man of her dreams on the platform at Hampstead Tube Station, finds out she is loved and makes friends with her sister-in-law

Honestly, I make myself laugh sometimes about other's astrological gullibility. I've picked up very little knowledge on the subject apart from which sign everyone I know is born under, but I know nothing about the qualities attached to each sign, compatibility of signs or anything, but I can bluff my way through, apparently convincingly. I find it very hard to accept that all people on the planet born in the same month in the whole history of mankind display similar characteristics.

To take it to its logical conclusion, does this mean that Hitler was simply displaying attributes of the Arian (Aryan?) sign? Could one go so far as to proclaim that all known tyrants were born in between 21 March and 20 April? That would give added weight to the old Nietzsche/nurture debate.

I once told Franny that her latest man was not a good bet as Cancerians were notoriously secretive. Of course, I'd just made that up. But even Franny, with her far superior knowledge on the subject, did not question me on this; per- haps I had got it right. Well, I did in that instance – his secret turned out to be a wife and three children in a huge house in Maidenhead. Ah well, there's Cancer men for you.

Am I witty, charming, intelligent and talented because I am a Gemini? Is Mother highly emotional and prone to tears because she is Aquarian? Are all Capricorns like Simon – moody, fiercely loyal but given to change their minds without warning? As for Scorpios, if Dad is anything to go by, they are nice as pie one minute then hit you with one when you are least expecting it. This is quite difficult in a father.

But not as difficult as it was in a husband.

1993
Waiting for the script to arrive

I wake early. In all the homes Adam and I have shared together (three) we have always had the morning sun in our bedroom. And I always sleep on the window side. So I always wake early.

It's Saturday. The alarm will not go off and Adam will sleep till at least ten o'clock. The clock says 7.00. It's unlikely I will get back to sleep, so I lie there with my eyes closed for a while. Every so often I open them and look at the person with whom I have shared a bed for the last seven years. Even when he's asleep, he looks like shit.

His skin is pale, an unhealthy white. He doesn't look relaxed. He looks ill. His slim frame is on the verge of turning flabby. He is by no means overweight, but he is very very unfit. The lifeless hair on his head falls just short of his shoulders, and the hair on his body is similarly unanimated, as if bored with its existence.

I have not desired this body for some time. Social conditioning has, however, driven me to make use of it about once every six weeks or so. But always at my command.

I look down at my body. It's still in good shape. My lanky teenage years finally softened into a slight roundness around the bum and tum. But still no sign of a waist. My small breasts have remained firm and round despite never having had any support of any kind. I know this can't go on for ever, but for now I am exceedingly grateful. It's a good body. My lovers always used to tell me so.

Before Adam.

I don't think he ever told me.

I know I have wasted it. Not allowed it to live up to its potential. My body was made to be enjoyed. I look over again at Adam and feel the sadness of those wasted years. Then I feel the anger of neglect. Finally I know I have to do something about this.

How hard can it be to end a marriage?

∞

'This is the hardest thing I've ever had to say, but I have to say it. Then it will be real.'

I wait for Simon to continue.

'It's over. My marriage is over. There is absolutely no chance that Sadie and I will ever live together again. We have no future together. There, I've said it.'

He sinks back in his chair in relief.

The waiter appears to refill our glasses, emptying the last drops into Aidan's glass, who discreetly signals for another bottle.

I wonder why Simon has chosen this particular occasion to make his announcement. Kate, who has been expertly breastfeeding Baby Bardolph while simultaneously tucking into her linguini vongole, doesn't react. She doesn't look at me or at Simon. Aidan does his best not to show how uncomfortable he must be feeling and I am torn between crying, hugging Simon and asking the million and one questions that need answers after such a decision has been reached.

I look over at Kate, who still refuses to look at me. I realise that she must have known about this. She has been party to Simon's decision to give up the fight. I can almost hear her saying it, 'Let go of the dream, give up the fantasy. It's not going to happen.' Good old pragmatic Kate. Not thinking at all about her own position in this. I wish I could believe that.

I start to say something, then stop. I try again. I'm not really sure what to say. In the end I settle for, 'Are you all right?' and lean over to place my hand on Simon's.

'Yes,' says Simon, brighter and cheerier than I've heard him for a long time, 'I'm fine.'

The waiter reappears with the new bottle and takes our plates away.

Simon bangs both hands down on the empty space in front of him. 'So?' he says.

It seems incredibly difficult to resume normal conversation, so I excuse myself to head for the Ladies'. As I walk behind Aidan's chair he stretches out his arm so that his hand brushes me as I pass. Aidan. How can such tiny gestures bring such joy to my life?

When I return, normal conversation has resumed, as I hoped it would, and Simon and Aidan are discussing the merits of *Manhattan* over *Annie Hall*. Woody Allen – one of my favourite topics of conversation. I join in enthusiastically, but manage to bring the lunch to an embarrassing standstill by telling Simon that he will feel differently about *Husbands and Wives* now that his marriage is over and will appreciate the subtleties that were lost on him last time he saw it and declared it an inferior work.

'Well, that's a good reason to get divorced,' he says.

Kate, who has been mostly silent throughout all this, rises from her chair. 'Are you taking me home, Hattie?' she asks.

'Yes, yes of course I am.'

Aidan pays the bill while Simon and Kate whisper together, away from the table. I look at Aidan, who shakes his head at me with the warmest, most affectionate smile. 'It's a good job we all love you,' he says.

1977
You don't have to mean it

I kiss Adam goodbye at his front door. Toby has gone to the car.

'I'll call you tomorrow.'

'OK.'

I have started to walk towards Toby and the waiting car.

'I love you,' says Adam.

I stop. I turn around. But Adam has gone. I stare at the closed door. Toby honks the car horn. Slowly turning around, I try to get a grasp on what just happened. Where is Toby? I spot the car's headlamps about ten yards down the road and start to walk towards them. But everything feels different. My heart feels heavy whilst my head feels light. Is that a line from a song?

I get in the car. Toby says something. I don't hear it. He sounds like a chipmunk on acid.

Suddenly this extraordinary sound comes from my chest and out of my mouth.

'Are you all right?' asks Toby. 'What was that?'

'I don't know,' I say.

'Is that a new laugh you're developing, because if so, I don't think much of it.'

I try to find my old laugh. A high-pitched squeak comes out.

'What is up with you?'

'I feel a bit weird.'

'You weren't smoking, were you?'

'No.'

'So what is it, then?'

It feels ridiculous to think or feel this but I say, 'Adam loves me and everything feels weird.'

Toby says nothing, just manically cleans the inside of the windscreen with his tiny hand while changing gear with the other one. No hands on the wheel. But even Toby's daredevil driving can't scare me tonight.

Because somebody loves me.

I make that sound again.

'Are you sure you're all right?' asks Toby.

'I'll always love him. I'll never love anyone like I've loved him.'

Kate has stayed true to her word. We haven't talked about it much over the years. But it's always been there. Like we know that Kate is blond and pretty and talented and organised and caring, we know that she loves Simon. It's part of her make-up, part of what makes Kate Kate.

She's made it very difficult for herself to form other relationships because she has created a bench mark against which they will all be measured and they will then all necessarily fail. Because once someone finds that out, they will always feel second best, inadequate, compared and contrasted.

No other relationship she's had has managed to over-come this hurdle, because no one, least of all a man, wants to feel those things. However many good qualities these few men have had, their biggest failing has always been that they are not Simon.

And now it looks like she has got what she always wanted. In her quiet, practical way she has held out for her dream.

Passive-aggressive I think Woody Allen would call it.

1980
'Certain women should be struck regularly, like gongs'

Tom grabs me. Four of his fingers are pressing down hard on the top of my arm and his thumb presses down hard underneath. I know this will leave bruises as he has done so before.

It really hurts.

I try to shake him off. Then, when I realise he isn't going to let go, I calmly and quietly explain to him how I was on Rueben's bike for approximately ten minutes, how we drove up and down Ferme Park Road with its marvellous straight, steep hill and how Franny was waiting for us at the bottom and how I only wanted to know what it felt like to ride a motor bike because I'd never done it before.

'You fancy him, don't you?'

'Rueben?'

'Yes. Don't you?'

'No, I don't.'

'Don't lie to me.' He squeezes my arm a little harder.

'You're hurting me.'

'Admit you fancy him, then I'll let go.'

'I don't fancy him.'

'Then why did you go on the bike with him?'

'Because I wanted to.'

'You slut.' He lets go of my arm and pushes me onto the bed. I get up and walk towards the door. He comes behind me and grabs my other arm.

'Where are you going?'

'Home, of course.'

'We're supposed to be spending the evening together.'

'You must be joking,' I say.

'Why not?'

'Are you serious?'

'I need you to go over my lines with me.'

'Find someone else.'

He has both my arms now and has pulled me to face him. Then he gently, tenderly, beautifully, overwhelmingly, passionately kisses me on the mouth.

'Stay?' he pleads.

I stay.

1980
Be kind enough to glance between my shoulder blades

Someone comes lurching towards me. He looks like he's about to throw up. I dive into the nearest room. Grace's bedroom. Bodies are strewn all over the place. I can barely make out who is in there. The lights are out. One candle is lit and the air is blanketed in thick smoke. I leave the smoking room. I go next door to Kate's bedroom. Simon is playing his guitar to a mostly female audience. Kate is lying across him, resting her head against his thigh. He smiles at me. I smile back. I leave the music room.

Most people seem to be crowded into the hall, sitting on the stairs, drinking tasteless wine out of plastic cups, then using them as ashtrays. Upstairs, the sound of The Clash is boom-booming out of Simon's bedroom. He is the only one of us with a stereo.

I walk straight into gorgeous Gabe.

'I'm going,' he shouts.

'You can't,' I say. 'I've not said one word to you.'

'Where are the coats?' he asks.

'Upstairs, my room,' I shout.

'Where's Franny?' he asks. 'I want to say goodbye.'

'I haven't seen her for ages,' I say.

'Maybe she's gone,' shouts Gabe.

This is getting ridiculous. Gabe attempts to manoeuvre himself past me.

Come to think of it, I haven't seen Tom lately either.

'I'll get your coat,' I say. I know Gabe's coat. It's an old squirrel fur. He bought it off me.

'Besides,' I shout, 'I want to go upstairs. You never know what I might find.'

I open the door of my bedroom and sure enough I find what I'm half expecting to see – Franny and Tom mouth to mouth on my bed.

'You bitch!' I scream at her, then dramatically turn and run down the stairs. Naturally my progress is impeded by the amount of people hanging around on them, but I manage to make it into the street.

Franny is right behind me.

'How could you?' I ask. 'You're not interested in Tom. You know you're not. And my bed. How could you do it on my bed?'

Franny is silent.

'No excuse,' she says. 'Don't hate me.'

I glare at her. I don't hate her.

∞

As I am never late, I never have to rush anywhere, so I leisurely make my way towards the ticket office. The man in front of me is renewing his season ticket, so I settle in for a stress-free wait and turn to watch the steady stream of travellers emerge like spring bulbs from underground as they near the top of the escalator.

Then I see him.

My first thought is, he looks cold. I stare hard as the picture of Tom comes into focus.

Skin – blue. Eyes – without focus. Cheeks – hollow. Hair – used to be a good point but now lank, neglected. Lips – once full, rich and frighteningly red, now dry, cracked and sore.

He passes me; barely one foot separates us. I automatically flinch in the memory of what close contact often led to. He notices nothing around him but gently sways on his way.

1988
Simon's got it bad

'I've met the most fantastic woman.'

I know this must be serious because Simon is prone to describing the female sex as girls. But my next thought is for Kate.

'Oh? Who?' I try to sound interested.

'Sadie.'

I laugh.

'What's so funny?'

'"Miss Sadie Thompson"?'

Simon laughs too.

'I hadn't thought of that,' he says.

'So who does she look like? Gloria Swanson, Joan Crawford or Rita Hayworth?'

'More of the Sigourney Weaver, I think.'

'Are you serious?'

'Well, she's tall, slim, athletic-looking with short dark hair.'

'So is Linford Christie.'

'I'll ignore that.'

'So where'dya meet her?'

'You know Toby wanted me to take some pictures of him at this Charity do he was performing at?'

'Oh, yes.'

'There.'

'What was she doing there?'

'She was one of the organisers. She works for some women's charity, you know, women's refuge, battered wives, refugees, advice centre, you know the sort of thing.'

'That's very specific. You were obviously paying a lot of attention to what she was saying.'

'Actually, I couldn't take my eyes off her breasts.'

'Simon!'

'Just teasing.'

'No you weren't. Anyway, how did Toby get involved in all that?'

'You know Toby – he doesn't care where he's asked to perform. He'll sing at the opening of a bag of crisps.'

'Sadie, huh? I can just see her. Lots of silver jewellery, big beads, no make-up, Indian cotton skirt, embroidered top; Ms-wishy-washy-liberal-goody-two-shoes. All sandals and sprouts. That's not you.'

'Actually, she's not like that at all. She's Australian.'

'Did I miss something?'

'I'm seeing her tonight.'

'That was quick work. When do I meet her?'

'I have the feeling you're not taking this terribly seriously.'

'You only met her yesterday.'

'True. But sometimes you just know, you know?'

I wish I knew that feeling, but I don't.

1991
These are my requirements

It's time to have Helena over for dinner again. This doesn't happen very often. The strain is too great. If we invite Helena, we must also ask Julian and Melanie and then we can get it over with in one go.

I worry about these meals for far longer than I should. I worry about how the house looks, how clean it is, where I buy the food from, how fresh it tastes; will they mind if I buy a dessert instead of make one? All these things are really important to me not because I actually feel them, but because these are the things that Helena and Melanie care about and these are the things that will be commented upon if they do not adhere to their very high standards.

There is little point in discussing the menu with Adam; whatever I say he will suggest something else. He does that about everything.

He always has a better idea, an easier plan, an alternative arrangement. It's about feeling of some use, I think. But I don't make allowances for this, I just get irritated.

It takes about a week to prepare my life and the dinner.

They are late. They got lost. This is habitual on their visits. They are making some kind of point about not knowing their way around the N's of London as easily as they know their way around the NW's. I already feel inferior.

Helena offers the air either side of her cheeks. I place my kisses in the space provided.

Melanie is only slightly more affectionate. We brush cheeks and touch arms. She is warmer with Adam. Julian is reserved with me; polite, interested in the same way The Queen would be. He must know I have no warm feelings for him.

Adam offers drinks. If he has learned anything from Helena it is how to be the perfect host. He provides grandly and generously. I make noises in the kitchen. These are frowned upon. I am the only member of the Levy extended family that cooks and serves her own meals. I am lacking in the hostess department because of this.

Adam and Julian talk shop. Helena and Melanie discuss Knightsbridge. I feel like the hired help who has the audacity to sit at the same table as her employers. I have no small bell to ring to summon the next course. My largest faux pas is I have no dining room. We eat around the large kitchen table. Thus I have learned the art of clearing up dinner parties as I go along, deliberately sparing my guests the sight of dirty pans, pots and plates. Helena has been seated facing away from the cooking area to be doubly spared the unwelcome view.

Harvey must be locked in the bedroom during dinner. Dogs are prone to laddering stockings in their excitement. This cannot be risked. So on top of everything, I have to put up with a sulking Whippet.

My cooking tastes woefully inadequate. The plates are pottery not bone china; the glasses are thick and green not crystal and clear; the cutlery is stainless steel not silver; the napkins, horror of all horrors, are paper not cloth; and the food feels heavy, juice laden, piled on plates not arranged nouvelle-like neatly and cleanly. I don't tie my French beans together, or ribbon my carrots or fan out pink slices of duck. I don't even decorate the table. If the season allows, I may cut a few flowers from the garden and put them in a small vase in the centre. But this is not a priority. Clearly I have much to learn.

No one drinks too much; no one eats too much. We retire to the lounge for coffee and . . . Shit! I forgot to buy chocolates. Fortunately Melanie came armed with a large box of the most sought-after, desirable Belgian variety and I am forced, against acceptable behaviour, to open these.

The evening is almost over. What exactly did I achieve? Helena is as pained as ever, Julian as cold, Adam as distant and Melanie as ridiculous.

How do I fit in to all this?

1977
Oh brave new world

We've never tasted anything like this in our entire lives. We've never eaten like this before. In the car. Stuffing our faces with this extraordinary mixture of bread, cheese, some kind of meat, gherkins, mayonnaise, tomatoes, tomato sauce and thin salt-heavy *chips and milkshakes so thick you can hardly suck them out of the straw.*

Suddenly food and the eating of it doesn't have to be a big deal anymore. We can eat on the way to a film or on the way out or on the way home or any goddamn time we like. Fast food has arrived and when Toby, Simon and I sit in Toby's car on the corner of Jermyn Street and Haymarket and bite into that first ever Big Mac, we are hooked; not just into the unique taste but the whole experience, the whole lifestyle that it offers.

It offers freedom.

Life will never be the same again.

1974
Something beginning with . . .

On the days that I'm feeling particularly dissatisfied, my only comfort is in doodling. Geography seems to trigger off alarming spates of doodling and my geography workbooks begin to resemble fantasy lands of my own creation. I have long since abandoned even a pretence of interest in the tin output of Chile or the square mileage of the lake areas of Central Africa or even the geological structure of the earth beneath London.

No. Geography is not for me.

One lesson which manages to reach previously undreamed of levels of uninterest finds me making elaborate shapes and patterns which all seem to stem from the letter 'R'. I am having a wonderful time. Sub-Beardsleyesque designs flow from my pen. Medieval monks hard at work at their illuminated scripts would have hailed my work as genius. I am unstoppable until Mr Muldoon on walkabout around the classroom spots that my drawings bear little resemblance to the Maldives and requests my presence in the staffroom at lunchtime.

I don't care. Like I said, Geography and me don't get on – don't need to get on.

Margie grabs me as the exceedingly irritating pips that mark the end of lessons burst out of the tannoy system.

'What did Mouldy Old Dough say?'

'He wants me to go to the staffroom at lunchtime.'

'Creep.'

'Yeah.'

'Are you coming down the club tonight?'

'I don't know. I've got some homework to do.'

'How are you ever going to get anyone to fancy you if you keep your nose in books all the time?'

I shrug my shoulders.

'I don't think I feel like it tonight.'

'I think you should come. I think you might meet someone tonight.'

'Why do you say that?'

Then I remember my doodles.

But before I can speak Margie says, 'Someone whose name begins with—'

' "R",' we both say together.

We are spooked into silence. Eventually Margie says, 'How did you know that?'

'That's what I've been doodling in my exercise book.'

I show her my work.

'That's it. You have to come.'

'Isn't Paul going tonight?'

'No, he's playing football.'

I get it. Someone has to look after her handbag while she dances.

I ponder the delights of Margie, boyfriend-free for the evening, on the prowl and not desiring my company.

'Be vivid,' she once told me, confusing the word with its opposite.

I make a decision to defy the fates and stay at home re-reading Northanger Abbey.

I'll never know whether that was a good decision or not.

1975
Once upon a dream

I can see him very clearly. He has the most beautiful eyes. They are small but blue and clear and deep and his very soul shines out of them. His hair is black and thick and curly; his skin white, but his cheeks show a healthy rosy glow. He has a fine nose, a noble nose and my most favourite kind of mouth; the one that has no middle dent in the top lip, it simply curves across the face like a rainbow.

I fall in love with him in my dream and wake feeling happier than I can remember, then cross that it was not real. I try to fall asleep again to get him back, to get the feeling back. But I fail.

Who is he?

Mother is calling for me. She's taking me shopping for boots.

The shock is too much. From him to Mother in less than five minutes is very difficult to bear. I don't think I've woken up properly.

I dress in a daze. Then Mother makes me get changed. It's not sensible to wear trousers if we're looking for boots. Unfortunately she's right. So I change into one of my new 'old' suits. Mother is not happy about this. She doesn't understand the attraction for old clothes. Especially the sort of clothes that she loathed wearing when she was young.

I skip breakfast and we leave the house. Normally we get the bus from the bottom of the hill straight to Oxford Street, but Mother has decided to travel to town on the tube. I just follow submissively, wishing that either I was back in bed asleep, happy and in love, or on my own with one of Mother's blank cheques.

In the dank, dark of the underground tunnel that takes us to the Northern Line South platform, I scuff my toes and watch the ground as I scrape over it.

'Pick your feet up,' says Mother, as she has done every day of my life since I put my first foot in front of the other and walked. 'It's no wonder you go through your shoes so quickly.'

The platform is empty except for a young couple on a bench halfway down. I tell Mother we should walk further along so that when we get off at Euston to change we will be directly opposite the exit.

Sauntering slowly down the dirty concrete, I fix my eyes on the couple on the bench. As we get nearer, the boy's features come into focus. I had already spotted the black curly hair, but then I see the white skin, the rosy cheeks, the noble nose, the arched lip. When he looks up at me and I see into his soul, I know he has recognised me. But we are not alone. I am with Mother. He is with . . . someone. This is not our time.

But we know that we exist for each other. And that will have to do. There will be comfort in that, sometimes.

I saw the man of my dreams on the platform at Hampstead Tube Station.

I have never seen him again.

Not even in my dreams.

∞

'Is it a sign of getting old, do you think?'

'What?'

Much as I love Franny, I do wish that she listened a little more attentively and I didn't have to repeat everything at least twice.

'You know. Not fancying as many men as you used to?'

'Speak for yourself.'

'I used to think that if you put me anywhere, you know, any gin joint in any town in all the world, there'd be someone I'd want to go to bed with.'

'That's because you're a slut.'

'Says the Mother of all Sluts.'

Franny flushes the toilet and appears from the bathroom. I am sitting on the floor outside the open door.

'You don't get it, do you?'

'What?'

I follow her into the kitchen, where she attempts to light the gas to boil the kettle to make us a cup of tea with a tea bag that she will no doubt fish out from the many half-used packs of different teas that litter the work surface next to the hob. Finally successful, she turns to me.

'It's not because you're getting older. It's because you're feeling settled.'

'Oh.' She's on that kick again. I don't want to play ball, so I change the subject.

'When's Phil back from LA?'

She doesn't answer immediately, but surely I notice a slight stiffening of her shoulders and a tightening of the lips.

'I'm not sure.'

'Franny?'

'He might not come back.'

'What?' Now I'm making her repeat something that I heard perfectly well the first time. 'Why didn't you say something before?'

'It's fine,' she says, 'that's why. After all, there's still Greg.'

'But Greg isn't Phil, as you well know.'

'No, no he's not. But he is Greg. And I adore him.'

'So what's with Miss LA-LA then? Is he staying to be with her?'

'Ironically, one of the reasons he went over there was to finish it.'

'But—'

'Oh no, he did. He did finish it. But he's decided it's time for a change. Wants to do something completely different. He's asked me to go over.'

'Franny! I can't believe you haven't mentioned any of this.'

'I know. I just feel I've made such a fucking mess of everything. I know no one approves of what I've been doing—'

'It's not about approval. It's nobody's business what you do. As long as you're happy, that's all that matters.'

'The awful thing is ... Oh God, it's so awful I can't bear it—'

'What? What's awful?'

We are interrupted by the kettle piercing the air with its whistle. It's so loud it could be announcing the arrival of a steam train. Franny turns it off.

'Tell me what's so awful.'

'I . . . I don't want only one of them. I want them both. That's the whole point.'

'I knew that.'

'You did?'

'Of course I did. What do you think?'

'I thought you thought I just couldn't make up my mind between them. I thought that's what everyone thought.'

'No.'

'Oh.'

'Does that make it any better?'

'No.'

She turns to the tea and reaches for a bag out of a box that says 'Decaffeinated Earl Grey', but that is not what it looks like, smells like or tastes like.

'Don't worry about what anyone else thinks. What do you want to do?'

'I want them both here. Like it was before. I don't want to live in LA. Can you imagine me there?'

Of course not. Franny is strictly a cold weather girl. The more layers she can wear, the happier she is. Waistcoats, cardigans, jackets, shawls, hats – she loves them all, and wears them all, preferably at the same time. No. Franny would not suit LA.

'It's that changes thing again,' I tell her.

'I know. It's so annoying.'

I laugh at her choice of word. Only Franny, dear

Franny, would describe life's upheavals, the roller-coaster ride we are all on, the obstacle course we have to negotiate, as 'annoying'.

'Time to move on, I guess.'

We drink our unrecognisable tea in silence until Franny remembers she has the remains of a chocolate cake. Somewhere.

1988
Obviously not as unique as I thought

It's amazing how many people think Sadie and I are sisters. Far more than ever believe it is Simon and me that are related. No one said anything about it at first. I think it was Dad that put into words what had crossed my mind, fleetingly, ridiculously, I thought.

'Sadie's not unlike you, you know.'

'Hmmm.' I answer.

I don't want to see it. First of all, I don't want to believe that there is anyone who is 'Like Me', physically or in temperament. I am not a type. Only other people are types. There is no one 'Like Me'. I am unique.

Wrong. Sadie is 'Like Me'.

'We don't have the same hair,' I tell Dad.

'You don't have the same hair style,' he corrects me.

'We don't wear the same clothes,' I tell Dad.

'You have better taste than her,' he compliments me.

'We don't have the same sense of humour,' I tell Dad.

'She's Australian,' he reminds me.

I like Sadie enormously. She's interesting and clever and funny

247

and wise. She's confident and ambitious and motivated and sexy. And I can totally understand why Simon has fallen in love with her.

Dad adores her. Mother finds it difficult to find things to talk to her about. It's hardly surprising. Mother is remarkably uninformed on Women's issues. She still talks about ' "Women's Lib" being a load of nonsense.' I sometimes half expect to find her sitting by the fireside darning socks. It's Dad's fault. He's protected her from the world. She doesn't need to know how to do anything that he can do for her. That's how it is and that's obviously how he wanted it and she likes it.

It is Sadie that points all this out to me. But then Sadie has made a life study of lifestyles of women. Sadie is generous towards Mother's retarded outlook and gently encourages me to leave her alone. But it's too late for that. Besides, I blame the Daily Mail, not Dad.

It's obvious from quite early on that Sadie is going to work wonders on all of us.

Except for Adam, of course. He is beyond help.

1989
Stop me if I'm interfering

'I like Adam.'

'You do?'

'Why do you sound so surprised?'

'Well, I just assumed you didn't.'

Sadie laughs. It is one of her more unfortunate features. Sadie laughs like Woody Woodpecker.

I attempt to talk over it in order to cease the grating sound that is making my bones quiver.

'I shouldn't really be surprised. One of Adam's talents is getting people to like him. I thought that maybe you might have seen through it.'

'He is very likeable.'

'Yes, I know. Like I said, he's very good at it.'

'But he's not really likeable?'

'No, I don't mean that. Obviously he is, if everybody likes him.'

'You must like him.'

I have to think about this.

'Well, yes. There are lots of things I like about us, our life.'

'That's not the same as liking him.'

I can't believe I'm having this conversation. I've known Sadie barely three months. I've known Adam for fifteen years.

'Of course I like Adam. We live together. We have a great life.'

'OK,' says Sadie. 'That's great. I'm pleased you're happy.'

A pause.

'Have you tried therapy?'

I make a noise that is supposed to be a sort of laugh.

'I'm sorry,' she says. 'It's none of my business. I always do this. I think everyone should have therapy. It's been so good for me. I'd never have been able to fall in love with Simon without it.'

'Really?'

'Really. Look forget it. I'm a fan, that's all. I want to spread the word. Forget it. OK?'

'OK.'

But she's made me uneasy and I don't know whether to thank her for it or not.

I need to buy new glasses; the drinking-out-of variety.

The last time more than four people were in my flat wanting a glass of wine, I was crawling around in the cupboard under the stairs searching for a box of yet to be unpacked wine glasses that I'm sure was put there. My search was fruitless, well glassless anyway. So it will have to be a trip to the IKEA sale in order to replenish my glass-free cupboards and save the embarrassment of serving gorgeous pink sparkling Californian wine in the toothpaste glass like Liza Minelli in *Cabaret*.

But on the scheduled day I am suddenly and unexpectedly lumbered with both my niece and nephew to amuse for several hours. Never fear. IKEA is equipped with a play area for young tots to exhaust themselves in whilst their guardians spend hundreds of unnecessary pounds on cheap and cheerful unnecessary Swedish merchandise.

We queue at the entrance to the play area, but when it is our turn we discover to the horror of us all that Rufus does not fulfil the height requirement for entry. Hannah has a tantrum as she does not want to be left alone, Rufus cries mainly because Hannah is, and I panic, imagining Rufus and Hannah let loose in the glassware department and the potential damage they could inflict.

Hannah is eventually persuaded to go and play, but not before I've accused the young girl in charge of practising a form of 'apartheight' against small children. Her blank face stares back at me and I wonder firstly why I bother and secondly how you can work in IKEA without a sense of humour.

Chapter Twelve

In which our heroine lives almost happily ever after

Oh my God, oh my God, oh my God!

I received a phone call from Aidan to let me know that Luke has a spot on Adam's chat show and how did I feel about that?

I tried to be very adult and calm and professional and tell him that it was of no consequence that my new boyfriend has set up my old boyfriend to be interviewed by my ex-husband. Hey! That's Show Biz!

Aidan (can't imagine why or how) picked up something from my tone that informed him I was not totally comfortable with the situation. But I tried very hard to persuade him that everyone had a living to make, that's all in the past, it doesn't matter, it's not as if they are going to be talking about me, is it? I think Aidan was persuaded, but inside I'm all in a fluster.

My calm, rational side (do I actually have one?) is telling me that this has nothing to do with me whatsoever. But why do I feel so betrayed by Aidan? He should be having nothing to do with Adam and his career; he shouldn't be offering up his clients as potential guests on Adam's show. He should be sabotaging the programme, bad-mouthing Adam in the industry and making sure he never works again.

Of course he shouldn't be doing that.

But somewhere inside me I truly believe that those who care about me must make a stand on the situation (even four years later when they didn't even know me or Adam then). In other words, they must be on my side. They must agree with me that Adam is a selfish, loathsome liar and cheat who doesn't deserve anything good to happen in his life.

Sometimes I don't think those things at all. But I really really don't want my new life to have anything to do with my old life, otherwise all the old feelings will start to seep back in.

I don't think that's too unreasonable a demand.

1993
Where do we go from here?

'Have you spoken to Adam?'

Toby looks uncomfortable.

'I saw him the other night.'

'Oh. Did he say anything about anything?'

'No. No, of course not. If I didn't know it from you, I would never know that anything had changed in his life. He was just the same old Adam.'

'Did you say anything to him?'

'No.'

'Oh.'

'But I will. I mean I'll have to. How can I not?'

Exactly. How can he not?

'How did he look?'

'You know, the same.'

'And he never said a word about all this?'

'He asked how you were.'

'And what did you say?'

'I said you were fine.'

'Is that all?'

'Yes, that's all. That's all that was said.'

'So what did you talk about then?'

'You know. Stuff. You know Adam.'

And I know Toby, who was probably more concerned with telling Adam about his latest failed audition or hopeful conversation with a producer or having new photos taken, as Toby seems to do more frequently than any other actor I know. And then they probably had a couple of beers, smoked a joint, had some coke and watched some boy's film and the fact that Adam was living in a rented, one-room shithole flat without me, without Harvey and without all the trappings of his former life, would never have once featured in their conversation.

Or their concerns.

I find this very hard.

1993

There's that pain between my shoulder blades again

The phone rings.

'Hello?'

'Hiya.'

'Grace!'

'How are you doing?'

'All right. How are you?'

'Good.'

'How's Jan?'

'Oh, she's fine. She's away at the moment.'

'Oh. Where?'

'Some Greek island. She's running one of her therapy workshops, you know, for "Women Who Read Too Much".'

I laugh. 'You are mean.'

Pause.

'So, is everything all right? Have you sold the house yet?'

'Almost. Just waiting for those things that seem to take for ever.'

'Yes. Well that's good. So when will you move?'

'About a month. Should be in my new flat just after the New Year.'

'New Year, new start.'

'Yes.'

I am waiting to discover the reason for this phone call. It surely can't be simply in the name of concern. I know Grace has been seeing, socialising with Adam and Toby. Should I say something, or not?

'I appreciate you phoning,' *I tell her.*

'Oh,' *she replies.* 'Listen. I just wondered if, while you were *packing your stuff, you've come across a programme of The Threepenny Opera. You know, the one we did at college? I, er, need some information from it.'*

What is she talking about?

'I'll have a look and let you know.'

'Thanks.'

'Bye then.' I put the phone down.

I am in shock for a while. There always was something difficult in my friendship with Grace. And after I got together with Adam she made it perfectly clear whose company she preferred. But now I feel unclean and violated because I don't understand how anyone, especially those who once called themselves my friends, can so blatantly and humiliatingly abandon me for Adam.

I always said that there was no room on the fence. People had to make a choice. No one could successfully maintain independent friendships with both of us. It was just not possible. But the fact that they could choose Adam, thereby condoning his behaviour, was baffling to me.

Adam needed to be punished.

He won't be though, will he?

1974
She wishes for the cloths of heaven

I manage to find homes for all three of Bernice's kittens. She is very grateful, though a trifle concerned that undoubtedly they will have their names changed from Oisin, Iseult and Aedh (Bernice is a big fan of Yeats) to Tiddles or Kitty or Mitzi. But this is a minor upset in a move that allows her to stay on in my father's flat. She always refers to it as 'your father's flat', as if it is not really her home.

Well, it isn't. Ireland is her home. More specifically Sligo, hence the affiliation to all things Yeatsian, and she talks long, dreamily and romantically about her homeland.

I manage to find an excuse to visit her about every ten days or so. Mother starts to complain that my clothes are smelling of Bernice. Simon tells me that I am beginning to smell 'mad'.

I don't understand why he thinks Bernice is mad.

He says it's simply because of her smell. No sane person would deliberately make themselves smell like that.

I disagree.

Mother finally flips her lid when I come home from Bernice's, which is only a very small detour on the way home from school, bearing her gift to me of her old squirrel coat.

The smell of disintegrating (stoned) squirrel is really too much for Mother and she insists I throw it out. I refuse. She shouts and screams. I scream and cry and run up to my room declaring hatred for, and wishing instant annihilation on, anyone who isn't Bernice or Glyn or me and my squirrel coat. Naturally, no one understands me.

Simon can't understand why they bother with me. He thinks they are up to something like trying to lure me into some strange cult full of smelly people. He goes around the house bowing before me walking backwards repeating, 'Hail, O Smelly One!'

I kick him in the balls.

Bernice and Glyn are nice to me. That's why I go; because they don't treat me like a child, or an annoying little sister, or a chaperone to be left in the cloakroom and collected when the ball is over (as Margie is wont to do), or a machine that must produce intelligent essays on the significance of Jane Austen's lack of reference to the outside world, or perfect French translations. They treat me like someone they like.

And when they do a runner in the middle of the night owing Dad eight weeks' rent and leaving behind a pungency that no amount of recarpeting and redecorating seems to diminish, I enter my first great depression.

1987
Hello stranger (3)

I go into the small sandwich bar just off the Strand. I like to have time to do nothing before I go into the theatre. I don't like leaving home, arriving in town and going straight to the theatre. I think it's something about not wanting to make it feel like a job; taking away the monotony of repeating the same lines and doing the same moves, expressing the same reactions night after night after night. Sometimes it feels like factory work. So if I do something different each day, then I can break the routine. A little.

I like this sandwich bar. It is mirrored all the way around and high stools are placed in front of the small bar that runs around the room. The tables are placed in the centre. There are only three of them and today only one of them is occupied.

I collect my cappuccino from the counter and sit on one of the stools. I can see the back of, the face of, the back of the face of, disappearing into infinity into the depths of the reflected mirrors, a craggy-faced, saggy-eyed, well-lived, middle-aged man. There is intense beauty in the sadness he emits. In slow movements he takes a cigarette, Gauloise of course, from a packet, puts it in the side of his mouth and lights it with a match. I can't take my eyes off him.

He looks up and stares at the reflection of me.

'If this were a foreign movie,' I think to myself, 'the next scene would be us in bed together.'

But in real life you have to make contact, risk rejection, somehow work up to that moment.

And anyway – I have a show to do.

1996
Bull's-eye

'I've got something to tell you.'

Kate and I are sitting on the hill by the lake at Kenwood.

I look to her. She smiles.

'You're pregnant.'

She doesn't stop smiling.

'Oh, my God.' We fall into each other's arms.

'Well, that didn't take long.'

'No,' she says. 'But then I've never seemed to have a problem conceiving. I'm sorry,' she adds.

'Forget it,' I say, really meaning it. 'Another lifetime. But this is great. Does Mike know yet?'

'No. I'm seeing him later. I'll bet he'll be pleased it worked first time. It was a little weird.'

'Do you think things will change with you and him, now that it's actually happened?'

'No. I hope not. No. It will be fine. We've been friends for years. He's not going to go all domestic on me. We've talked it

*over and over. We'll both have the best of both worlds. I'll have
support when I need it and he can be as little or as much of a
hands-on father as he wants. If he doesn't want, it's fine; if he
does, great.'*

*'I hope it works out that easily. What happens when you fall
in love?'*

*Kate gives me her wistful, determined look, the one that went a
long way towards winning her that BAFTA. I try to swallow the
laugh that is rising in my throat. But she is not a Thomas Hardy
heroine now. She is just Kate sitting on a hillside, pregnant, having
achieved phase one of her master plan.*

'You know you did this last time.'

Simon gives Hannah a big push.

'No,' she squeals, 'that's too high.'

'No such thing,' says Simon pushing her again.

I am sitting on the swing next to Hannah, holding
Rufus on my lap. My feet don't leave the ground, but I
gently sway back and forth. Rufus seems content with
the arrangement.

'What?' asks Simon.

'Not tell me about you and Kate.'

'Too high,' says Rufus. I give him a squeeze.

'Oh,' is all he says. 'But you know it all from Kate.
She's your best friend. You're not going to hear anything
new from me.'

'Except how you feel about it.'

'I think it's pretty bloody obvious how I feel about
it.'

I make an irritated growling sound.

'Men!'

'I'm not "Men". I'm your brother.'

'Well don't act like them then.'

'Daddy! Daddy! Push me more.'

'Kate,' says Rufus.

'What is it about talking that you don't like?'

'I talk.'

'You know what I mean.'

'Actions speak louder than words.'

'Bollocks.'

'What are "bollocks" Daddy?'

'Never mind, Hannah. Your aunt has a very limited vocabulary.'

'What's a "limited vocabulary"?'

'Hattie, would you like to explain this one.'

'Sure. It means, sweetie, that some people who can't express themselves in words think that it's better to do it through actions. You know, like if you're angry with someone, instead of being able to tell them you're angry, you hit them, which isn't very clever is it?'

'Or,' says Simon, 'if you can't tell someone that you love them, you give them lots of kisses and cuddles.'

'Kisses and cuddles are good though, aren't they?'

'Of course they are. But so are words. Words are really important.'

'Bollocks,' says Rufus.

'You know, we never used each other's names.'

'What do you mean?' Kate asks, deftly wiping Baby Bardolph's tiny creases with the smallest piece of warm water-soaked cotton wool.

'I never used his name unless I was talking about him to someone else. I'd hardly ever have the need to call his name.'

'I'm sorry, but I don't understand. If he was upstairs and the phone rang for him, then you'd have to call him.'

'Yes. So I'd just say, "Phone for you." I wouldn't call "Adam! There's a phone call for you."'

'I still don't know what you're getting at.'

'I think it's significant, that's all, you know, that I could never use his name.'

'What did he call you?'

'Nothing. "Darling" sometimes. But he hardly used my name either.'

'You don't use my name very much.'

'Don't I?'

'Not really.'

'Oh. Then maybe it's something I just don't do. I never thought about it before. Except about Adam.'

'It doesn't matter now. It's been a long time.'

'I know. But sometimes you think about things. The silly things. The things that you should have taken more notice of when you were in it so you could have saved yourself a lot of the anguish and despair.'

'You were in denial.'

'No, I wasn't.'

Kate smiles.

'You don't miss a trick do you?'

'Happy?' I ask her out of nowhere.

'Where did that come from?'

'I don't know. I was just watching you and BB—'

'I wish you wouldn't call him that.'

'Apparently he's privileged that I call him anything at all.'

Kate laughs. Well, it's half a laugh really. The first part of Kate's laugh is always silent; she'll catch her breath three or four times and then a deep breath in will force her throat to vibrate, producing a kind of death rattle sound which leads to a deep sigh. But it's not always necessary to hear Kate laugh. Her eyes are always laughing.

'Yes,' she says. 'Of course I'm happy.'

1991
We all pat the dog

'I've got a job.'

'Really? I didn't know you were looking.'

'Of course I've been looking.'

'I thought you were making a go of the photography. You've been really busy – you're doing something most days. I mean, I tell everyone you're a photographer. If anyone asks me, "What does your brother do?" I tell them you're a photographer.'

'Do you?'

Now I'm getting irritated.

'Of course I do.'

'I didn't know that.'

'What should I have been saying? That you're a loser, a waster, someone who can't find any direction in life? Yet another victim of *the idle middle classes, living off the state, bleeding the country dry having wasted his privileged education?'*

A momentary concern that I might actually believe what I am saying crosses Simon's face. Then I relax into a smile.

'Just kidding. It's only Dad that thinks that. Not me. So, what's the job?'

'It's with a small publishers – Cradle Press. They're starting me as editorial assistant but a vacancy for commissioning editor is coming up soon and I should be able to have that job.'

'Cradle Press? Don't know them. Oh, yes I do. Simon! They publish all those hideous staunch feminist tracts. God, this really aggressive rep comes into the shop. George loathes her. She's so pushy. We've never sold any of their stuff. George won't let her near the place anymore.'

'They are a specialist press.'

'This is something to do with Sadie, isn't it?'

Simon looks sheepish.

'I knew it! Isn't being a photographer good enough for her?'

I am equally shocked and disappointed in both Simon and Sadie. Sadie for being so manipulative and Simon for being so malleable.

'We'll need a steady income. I've got a family to think about supporting.'

'I just can't believe you'll be earning more working for some dodgy publishing outfit than you would doing the photography.'

'It's guaranteed though. And it's office hours, same as Sadie works. At the end of the day I come home and leave it all behind, not spend all night in the dark room. I want to be with Sadie and the baby, when it arrives. I want to be there.'

'Ignore me,' I say. 'I'm just jealous.'

Simon laughs.

'I do ignore you, most of the time.'

I kick him under the table.

'It's called the Cuckoo Wrasse.'

'Wow! Weird,' says Franny, vacuuming the last drops of vodka out of the ice in the bottom of her glass.

'I'll get more drinks.' Kate goes up to the bar. Franny watches her go.

'How long do you think it will take before she gets her figure back?'

'Funnily enough, it doesn't seem to be her primary concern,' I say. I know both Franny and I are thinking of the vain, exercise-obsessed, care-dieting Kate of yesteryear. But that was then.

'So, this fish with the bird name—'

'Yes. Well there's fifty females to every male.'

'Every straight, available male? That's better odds than we get.'

'But the brilliant thing is if something happens to the male in the pack, like he dies or gets eaten or whatever, the most dominant female turns herself into a male.'

'How?'

'I don't know. It's one of those nature things, you know the things females need to do to secure the survival of the species even when there are no males around.'

'Top fish!' says Franny and goes into her baby's chuckle.

Kate returns with Franny's vodka and lime, my gin and tonic and her own Guinness.

'What's so funny?'

I tell Kate about the Cuckoo Wrasse.

'Well it wouldn't do for you,' she tells Franny. 'Or you either, Hattie, for that matter.'

I feel a change in the atmosphere. Franny has perhaps had a few too many vodkas. She won't be judged by Kate.

'So, it's all right for you, Mrs-get-me-the-nearest-healthy-sperm-so-I-can-have-my-baby, but not for the rest of us who are still searching for . . . for . . .' she tails off. She has tears in her eyes. I put my hand over hers to stop it shaking.

'You've missed the point,' I tell them. 'It's about dealing with change, making it work for you, you know?'

Kate settles back; Franny's glare relaxes into a half-smile.

'A toast,' I say and raise my glass. 'The girls.'

We toast 'the girls'.

'Another one,' I say. 'To Men – the little dears.'

We toast the little dears and all agree that they have their uses.

Aidan is actually crying. He really is crying. Real tears. His eyes are all red and puffy and he blows his nose, a lot. After we've left the cinema and we're driving home he suddenly starts again.

Aidan is speeding and a police car flashes us.

Halfway through the demand for Aidan's licence, the policeman notices his tears.

'Are you all right, sir?'

'He's fine,' I tell the policeman. 'We've just been to see *Bambi*.'

The policeman's eyes glaze over and he appears all wistful for a moment. Then he recovers himself and says, 'Well, just watch your speed, sir.'

Aidan turns to me and smiles.

'That was brilliant,' he says.

'The power of Disney,' I tell him.

We drive on in silence.

'I don't know. It gets me every time,' Aidan suddenly says.

'But you didn't cry when everyone else cries, you know in the "Your mother can't be with you anymore" bit.'

'No. It's the father stuff.'

Aidan has never mentioned his father before.

'You've not mentioned your father before.'

'No.'

There is a silence. Then Aidan starts to talk about his father.

I can almost forgive him for the Luke/Adam thing that I haven't yet had a chance to tackle him about. But that will have to wait. When a man starts to tell you about 'the father stuff', well, he may as well get out the ring and change his will then and there.

Rooting about amongst my boxes I come across the old Erté letters. I take them to the framer's and have them reframed the other way around. Now they hang above my new bed.

AH!

That's better.

Mother is terribly upset, as successfully predicted by Dad, about Simon and Sadie. She really doesn't know what to do to help. So she slips a disc.

I take this to mean that she is more upset about Simon and Sadie separating than she was about Adam and me, because when we separated she only had a severe attack of hay fever, which did nearly develop into asthma, but was not nearly so incapacitating as a slipped disc.

Naturally, everyone is expected to rally round and nurse her, but what actually happens is that she is pretty much left to her own devices flat on her back and Simon and I entertain Dad, making sure he is well fed, cooking for him or having some really fun meals out.

Mother makes an alarmingly speedy recovery.

Suddenly it is just the four of us again. It hasn't been just the four of us for years. Mother makes a brave attempt at Sunday lunch, which Simon and I make an even braver attempt to eat. After lunch Dad falls asleep in his armchair, Mother clears up alone and Simon and I watch *The Blue Veil* on the telly.

'This is one of the first films I ever remember seeing,' I tell Simon.

'How can you remember that?' he asks.

'You never forget the first time you see Joan Blondell.

I always aspired to her unique combination of worldliness and vulnerability. Even at five years old.'

'Don't be silly.'

I am being silly. We are not five and eight. We are thirty-seven and forty. And we've had broken marriages and strange love affairs and children and dogs and belonged to other families. And we've had different homes and different jobs and different friends. And now, even though we are both relatively content with new, or in Simon's case old, partners, this is where we always come back to. Because this is where nothing changes – watching the Sunday afternoon movie whilst Dad sleeps in his armchair and Mother bangs about in the kitchen.

Epilogue

❦

The phone rings.

'Hello.'

'There's been a change—'

'I'll be right there.'

I put down the phone and check the clock; 1.13 the numbers tell me. I watch the flashing red dots for a few seconds, then sleepily drop out of bed.

I open cupboards and drawers in a daze. I have no idea what I am wearing.

The figure in the bed stirs. There is warmth and comfort in its presence. I lean over and breathe in the love which touches me even in his sleep. One beautiful green eye opens.

'Was that the phone?'

'I have to go to the hospital.'

Aidan sits up.

'I'll drive you.'

'No. I'm all right. Stay here and sleep. I'll call you later.'

He kisses me lightly on the mouth.

'This is it,' I say.

There's no answer to be made, so he just smiles and mouths 'Bye.'

'I love you,' I tell him.

The road is busier than it should be at this time of the morning and panic rises with every red light.

I park sticking out from a double yellow line, then dash along the familiar route to the room on the twelfth floor.

Simon is in the corridor.

'That was quick,' he says.

'Was it? How is he?'

'The nurse said it could be anytime now.'

'Shit,' I say.

Mother comes out of the room.

'The nurse is just changing the sheets,' she tells me coolly, calmly, unemotionally.

When the nurse comes out, we file into the room.

Dad lies half sitting up, propped by half a dozen pillows. But then he always sleeps like that. His eyes are closed. His arms lie by his side on top of the sheets.

He doesn't look like he's about to die.

'He doesn't look like—' I start to say, but stop.

Dad opens his eyes.

'We're all here now,' Simon tells him.

'Good, good,' Dad murmurs. 'Now we can get organised.' His eyes close.

Mother sits on the left-hand side of the bed in front of the window. I sit on the other side on a low armchair where I've sat every time I've been to see him over the last fortnight. Simon hovers – sometimes perching on the end of the bed, sometimes sitting at the foot of it, but generally being only too glad to be sent on errands to fetch the nurse for either an explanation of a change in Dad's breathing patterns or for something for Mother to stop her feeling sick.

We sit like this for hours, watching Dad breathe.

The sky begins to lighten and I stare out of the window for a long time and watch the shape of Hampstead slowly become visible out of the darkness. Straight ahead and to the right, the trees of the Heath reveal themselves standing on top of each other as they climb towards Kenwood like a troupe of acrobats forming a human pyramid. To the left, the shops of the High Street appear like building blocks with the clock tower, which rarely tells the right time, balancing precariously on the top.

I wonder if Dad minds dying with a view North towards his dreaded suburbs instead of facing South towards his beloved West End.

It is half past eight. Simon volunteers to go and move all our illegally parked cars and to return with coffee and croissants.

There is no change in Dad.

Mother leaves the room and for the first time that night I am alone with my father.

I sit on the edge of the bed.

'It's all right to let go,' I tell him. 'You can go. Please go.' But not out loud. I say this as something between a thought and a speech. I want him to receive the message, but I don't want anyone else to know this is what I feel, even the people who aren't actually here right now.

When Mother returns I go to the toilet. On the door hangs a notice that must be signed by the cleaner every time the toilets are checked.

'For Week Ending 19 September,' it says at the top.

But all I can think of is, 'For Life Ending 19 September.'

By the time Simon returns there is a noticeable change in Dad's breathing. There is longer and longer between each breath and the breaths, when they do come, are shorter and shorter.

The nurse simply tells us that this is how it happens.

It takes about another hour.

We, who have been sitting here all night waiting for the moment, discover that there is no discernible moment of death.

When did it come? With the previous short breath or at some point in the long pause before the next one, which never arrived?

None of us moves.

None of us cries.

Dad looks exactly the same as he did when he was still – what – alive? But he's not.

A great calmness starts to emanate from the shape on the bed that was home to Dad for just past his biblically allotted time on earth. This was always his gift to us and now it pours out of him for us to grab and hold onto as if there will never be any more.

I get up to open the window. Mother looks at me and, with the smallest of head movements, nods her approval.

I stand by the open window. My mouth feels heavy. It is preparing my face for tears but a smile crosses it as quickly and briefly as the sudden break in the clouds of this overcast, drizzly Autumn morning, that brings a blinding strip of fluorescent sunlight flashing across the sky.

I turn back to the room to look at Dad. As I thought – he has gone. There is only a body left on the bed.

Simon offers to start making phone calls, so we leave Mother alone, each of us planting a small kiss on what was once Dad's forehead.

Outside in the corridor where the night began, Simon and I hug each other.

'Nothing stays,' he says and I feel my cheek become wet with my brother's tears.

'No,' I say. 'Nothing.'

A selection of other books from
Flame

Own Goals	Phil Andrews	0 340 74822 2	£6.99 ☐
My Legendary Girlfriend	Mike Gayle	0 340 71816 1	£6.99 ☐
Frozen Summer	Crysse Morrison	0 340 74865 6	£6.99 ☐
Bigtime	Marc Blake	0 340 71774 2	£6.99 ☐
The Cousin's Tale	Antonia Swinson	0 340 71694 0	£6.99 ☐

All Hodder and Stoughton books are available from your local bookshop or newsagent, or can be ordered direct from the publisher. Just tick the titles you want and fill in the form below. Prices and availability subject to change without notice.

Hodder & Stoughton Books, Cash Sales Department, Bookpoint, 39 Milton Park, Abingdon, OXON, OX14 4TD, UK. E-mail address: order@bookpoint.co.uk. If you have a credit card you may order by telephone – (01235) 400414.

Please enclose a cheque or postal order made payable to Bookpoint Ltd to the value of the cover price and allow the following for postage and packing:
UK & BFPO – £1.00 for the first book, 50p for the second book, and 30p for each additional book ordered up to a maximum charge of £3.00.
OVERSEAS & EIRE – £2.00 for the first book, £1.00 for the second book, and 50p for each additional book

Name _____

Address _____

_____

_____

If you would prefer to pay by credit card, please complete:
Please debit my Visa/Access/Diner's Card/American Express (delete as applicable) card no:

Signature _____

Expiry Date _____

If you would NOT like to receive further information on our products please tick the box. ☐